THE ENCHANTED MOCCASINS

and Other Native American Legends

Edited by
HENRY R. SCHOOLCRAFT

DOVER PUBLICATIONS, INC.
Mineola, New York

Bibliographical Note

This Dover edition, first published in 2007, is an unabridged republication of nineteen stories selected from *The Indian Fairy Book,* originally published by Frederick A. Stokes Company, New York, in 1916.

Library of Congress Cataloging-in-Publication Data

Schoolcraft, Henry Rowe, 1793–1864.
    [Indian fairy book. Selections]
    The enchanted moccasins : and other Native American legends / edited by Henry R. Schoolcraft.
        p. cm.
    "Unabridged republication of nineteen stories selected from The Indian fairy book, originally published by Frederick A. Stokes Company, New York, in 1916.
    ISBN-13: 978-0-486-46014-7 (pbk.)
    ISBN-10: 0-486-46014-2 (pbk.)
    1. Indians of North America—Folklore. I. Title.

E98.F6S37 2007
398.2089'97—dc22

2007008305

Manufactured in the United States of America
Dover Publications, Inc., 31 East 2nd Street, Mineola, N.Y. 11501

FOREWORD

These Indian fairy tales are chosen from the many stories collected by Mr. Henry R. Schoolcraft, the first man to study how the Indians lived and to discover their legends. He lived among the Indians in the West and around the Great Lakes for thirty years in the first part of the Nineteenth Century and wrote many books about them.

When the story-tellers sat at the lodge fires in the long evenings to tell of the manitoes and their magic, of how the little boy snared the sun, of the old Toad Woman who stole the baby, and the other tales that had been retold to generation after generation of red children, time out of mind, Mr. Schoolcraft listened and wrote the stories down, just as he heard them.

In 1856 this collection of his stories was published by Mason Brothers in New York City. A small brown book with quaint engravings for pictures, it is now only to be found here and there in families that have always treasured its delightful contents. It is republished, with revisions and with new illustrations in color, so that these stories may be passed on as they deserve.*

*This edition does not contain any color illustrations.

CONTENTS

THE BOY WHO SET A SNARE FOR THE SUN

AT the time when the animals reigned in the earth, they had killed all the people but a girl and her little brother, and these two were living in fear, in an out-of-the-way place. The boy was a perfect little pigmy, and never grew beyond the size of a mere infant; but the girl increased with her years, so that the task of providing food and shelter fell wholly upon her. She went out daily to get wood for the lodge-fire, and she took her little brother with her that no mishap might befall him; for he was too little to leave alone. A big bird of a mischievous disposition might have flown away with him. But at last she made a bow and arrows, and giving them to him said:

"My little brother, I will leave you behind where I have been gathering the wood; you must hide yourself, and you will soon see the snow-birds come and pick the worms out of the logs which I have piled up. Shoot one of them and bring it home."

He obeyed her, and tried his best to kill one, but he

came home unsuccessful. Then his sister told him that he must not despair, but try again the next day.

She accordingly left him again at the gathering-place of the wood and returned to the lodge. Toward nightfall she heard his little footsteps crackling through the snow, and he hurried in and threw down, with an air of triumph, one of the birds which he had killed.

"My sister," said he, "I wish you to skin it and stretch the skin, and when I have killed more, I will have a coat made out of the skins."

"But what shall we do with the body?" said she; for they had always up to that time lived upon greens and berries.

"Cut it in two," he answered, "and season our pottage with one half of it at a time."

It was their first dish of game, and they relished it greatly.

The boy kept on in his efforts, and in the course of time he killed ten birds—out of the skins of which his sister made him a little coat. Being very small, he had a very pretty coat, and a bird-skin to spare.

"Sister," said he one day, as he paraded up and down before the lodge, enjoying his new coat and fancying himself the greatest little fellow in the world—as he was, for there was no other besides him— "My sister, are we really alone in the world, or are we playing at it? Is there nobody else living? And tell me, was all this great broad earth and this huge big sky made for a little boy and girl like you and me?"

"Ah, no," answered the sister, "there are many others, but not harmless as you and I are. They live in a certain other quarter of the earth, and if we would not endanger our lives we must keep away from there. They have killed off all our kinsfolk and will kill us, too, if we go near where they are."

To this the boy was silent; but his sister's words only served to inflame his curiosity the more, and soon after he took his bow and arrows and went in the forbidden direction.

After walking a long time and meeting no one, he became tired and stretched himself upon a high green knoll where the day's warmth had melted off the snow. It was a charming place to lie, and he soon fell asleep. While he slept, the sun beat upon him. It not only singed his bird-skin coat, but so shrivelled and shrunk and tightened it on the little boy's body as to wake him up. And then when he felt how the sun had seared the coat he was so proud of, and saw the mischief its fiery beams had played, he flew into a great passion. He vowed fearful things, and berated the sun in a terrible way for a little boy no higher than a man's knee.

"Do not think you are too high," said he; "I shall revenge myself. Oh, sun! I will have you for a plaything yet."

On coming home he gave an account of his misfortune to his sister, and bitterly bewailed the spoiling of his new coat. He would not eat—not so much as a single berry. He lay down as one that fasts; nor did he move or change his manner of lying for ten full days, though his sister strove to prevail on him to rise. At the end of ten days he turned over, and then he lay full ten days on the other side.

When he got up he was very pale, but very resolute too. He bade his sister make a snare.

"For," said he, "I mean to catch the sun."

"I have nothing strong to make a snare of," objected the sister. But on his insisting, she brought forward a deer's sinew which their father had left, and soon made it into a string suitable for a noose. But the brother was not pleased with it; he told her that it would not do and directed her to find something else. She said she had nothing—nothing at all; but at last she thought of the bird-skin that was left over when the coat was made, and she wrought this into a string. And now the little boy was more vexed than before.

"The sun has had enough of my bird-skins," he said; "find something else."

She went out of the lodge, saying to herself, "Was there ever so obstinate a boy?" She did not dare to answer this time that she had nothing. Then luckily she thought of her own beautiful hair, and pulling some of it from among her locks, she quickly braided it into a cord, and, returning, handed it to her brother. The moment his eye fell upon the jet black braid he was delighted.

"This will do," he said, and he immediately began to run it back and forth through his hands as swiftly as he could; and as he drew it forth, he tried its strength. He said again, "This will do," and winding it in a glossy coil about his shoulders, he set out a little after midnight.

His object was to catch the sun before it rose. He fixed his snare firmly on a spot just where the sun must strike the land as it rose above the earth; and sure enough, he caught the sun, so that it was held fast in the cord and did not rise.

The animals who ruled the earth were immediately put into great commotion. They had no light; and they ran to and fro, calling out to one another and inquiring what had happened. They summoned a council to debate upon the matter, and an old dormouse, suspecting where the trouble lay, proposed that some one should be appointed to go and cut the cord. This was a bold thing to undertake, as the rays of the sun could not fail to burn whoever should venture so near to them.

At last the venerable dormouse himself undertook it, for the very good reason that no one else would. But all were glad to accept his offer, so he hastened to the spot where the sun lay ensnared.

Now at this time the dormouse was the largest animal in the world. When he stood up he looked like a mountain, and when he walked the earth trembled. His courage was great in proportion, but as he came nearer and nearer to the sun his back began to smoke and burn with the heat, and soon the whole top of his huge bulk was turned to enormous heaps of ashes. He succeeded, however, in cutting the cord with his teeth, and the sun, free, as round and beautiful as ever, rolled up again into the wide blue sky. But the dormouse—or blind woman as it is called—was shrunk away to a very small size; and that is the reason why it is now one of the tiniest creatures upon the earth.

The little boy returned home when he discovered that the sun had escaped his snare, and devoted himself entirely to hunting.

"If the beautiful hair of my sister would not hold the sun fast, nothing in the world could," he said. "I was not born, a little fellow like myself, to look after the sun. It requires one greater and wiser than I to regulate that."

So he went out and shot ten more snow-birds; for in this business he was very expert; and he had a new bird-skin coat made, which was prettier than the one he had worn before.

II

MANABOZHO, THE MISCHIEF-MAKER

THERE was never in the whole world a more mischievous busy-body than that notorious giant Manabozho. He was everywhere, in season and out of season, running about and putting his hand in whatever was going forward. To carry on his game, he could take almost any shape he pleased; he could be very foolish or very wise; very weak or very strong; very poor or very rich—just as happened to suit his humor best. Whatever any one else could do, he would attempt without a moment's reflection. He was a match for any man he met, and there were few manitoes that could get the better of him. By turns he would be very kind, or very cruel; an animal or a bird; a man or a spirit. And yet, in spite of all these gifts, Manabozho was always getting himself involved in all sorts of troubles; and more than once, in the course of his busy adventures, was this great maker of mischief driven to his wits' ends to come off with his life.

To begin at the beginning, Manabozho, while yet a youngster, was living with his grandmother near the edge of a wide prairie. It was on this prairie that he first saw animals and birds of every kind; he also there made first acquaintance with thunder and lightning; he would sit by the hour watching the clouds as they rolled, and musing on the shades of light and darkness as the day rose and fell.

For a stripling, Manabozho was uncommonly wide-awake. Every new sight he beheld in the heavens was a subject of remark; every new animal or bird, an object of deep interest; and every sound that came from the bosom of nature was like a new lesson which he was expected to learn. He often trembled at what he heard and saw.

To the scene of the wide open prairie his grandmother sent him at an early age to watch. The first sound he heard was that of the owl, at which he was greatly terrified. Quickly descending the tree he had climbed, he ran with alarm to the lodge.

"Noko! noko! grandmother!" he cried. "I have heard a monedo."

She laughed at his fears and asked him what kind of noise his reverence made. He answered:

"It makes a noise like this: Ko-ko-ko-ho."

His grandmother told him he was young and foolish; that what he heard was only a bird which derived its name from the peculiar noise it made.

He returned to the prairie and continued his watch. As he stood there looking at the clouds, he thought thus to himself:

"It is singular that I am so simple and my grandmother so wise; and that I have neither father nor mother. I have never heard a word about them. I must ask and find out.''

He went home and sat down, silent and dejected. Finding that this did not attract the notice of his grandmother, he began a loud lamentation, which he kept increasing, louder and louder, till it shook the lodge and nearly deafened the old grandmother. She at length said:

''Manabozho, what is the matter with you? You are making a great deal of noise.''

Manabozho started off again with his doleful hubbub; but succeeded in jerking out between his big sobs, ''I haven't got any father or mother; I haven't,'' and he set out again lamenting more boisterously than ever.

Knowing that he was of a wicked and revengeful temper, his grandmother dreaded to tell him the story of his parentage; as she knew he would make trouble of it.

Manabozho renewed his cries and managed to throw out, for a third or fourth time, his sorrowful lament that he was a poor unfortunate, who had no parents and no relations. Finally his grandmother said:

''Yes, you have a father and three brothers living. Your mother is dead. She was taken for a wife by your father, the West, without the consent of her parents. Your brothers are the North, East, and South; and being older than yourself, your father has given them great power with the winds, according to their names. You are the youngest of his children. I have nursed you from your infancy; for your mother, owing to the ill-treatment of your father, died when you were born. I have no relations beside you. Your mother was my only child, and you are my only hope."

"I am glad my father is living," said Manabozho. "I shall set out in the morning to visit him."

His grandmother would have discouraged him, saying it was a long distance to the place where his father, Ningabiun, or the West, lived.

This information seemed rather to please than to disconcert Manabozho; for by this time he had grown to such a size and strength that he had been compelled to leave the narrow shelter of his grandmother's lodge and to live out of doors. He was so tall that, as he stood up, he could have snapped off the heads of the birds roosting in the topmost branches of the highest trees, without being at the trouble to climb. And if he had at any time taken a fancy to one of the same trees for a walking-stick, he would have had no more to do than to pluck it up with his thumb and finger and strip down the leaves and twigs with the palm of his hand.

Bidding good-bye to his venerable old grandmother, who pulled a very long face over his departure, Manabozho set out at great headway, for he was able to stride from one side of a prairie to the other at a single step.

He found his father on a high mountain-ground, far

in the west. His father espied his approach at a great distance and bounded down the mountain-side several miles to give him welcome; and, side-by-side, apparently delighted with each other, they reached in two or three of their giant paces the lodge of the West, which stood high up near the clouds.

They spent some days in talking with each other—for these two great persons did nothing on a small scale, and a whole day to deliver a single sentence was quite an ordinary affair, such was the immensity of their discourse.

One evening Manabozho asked his father what he was most afraid of on earth.

He replied—"Nothing."

"But is there nothing you dread, here—nothing that would hurt you if you took too much of it? Come, tell me."

Manabozho was very urgent, and at last his father said:

"Yes, there is a black stone to be found a couple of hundred miles from here, over that way," pointing as he spoke. "It is the only thing earthly that I am afraid of, for if it should happen to hit me on any part of my body it would hurt me very much."

The West made this important circumstance known to Manabozho in the strictest confidence.

"Now you will not tell any one, Manabozho, that the black stone is bad medicine for your father, will you?" he added. "You are a good son, and I know you will keep it to yourself. Now tell me, my darling boy, is there not something that you don't like?"

Manabozho answered promptly—"Nothing."

His father, who was of a very steady and persevering temper, put the same question to him seventeen times, and each time Manabozho made the same answer—"Nothing."

But the West insisted—"There must be something you are afraid of."

"Well, I will tell you," said Manabozho, "what it is."

He made an effort to speak, but it seemed to be too much for him.

"Out with it," said Ningabiun, or the West, fetching Manabozho such a blow on the back as shook the mountain with its echo.

"Je-ee, je-ee—it is—" said Manabozho, apparently in great pain. "Yeo, yeo! I cannot name it, I tremble so."

The West told him to banish his fears and to speak up; no one would hurt him.

Manabozho began again, and he would have gone over the same make-believe of anguish, had not his father, whose strength he knew was more than a match for his own, threatened to pitch him into a river about five miles off. At last he cried out:

"Father, since you will know, it is the root of the bulrush."

He who could with perfect ease spin a sentence a

whole day long, seemed to be exhausted by the effort of pronouncing that one word, "bulrush."

Some time after, Manabozho observed:

"I will get some of the black rock, merely to see how it looks."

"Well," said the father, "I will also get a little of the bulrush-root, to learn how it tastes."

They were both double-dealing with each other, and in their hearts getting ready for some desperate work.

They had no sooner separated for the evening than Manabozho was striding off the couple of hundred miles necessary to bring him to the place where the black rock was to be procured, while down the other side of the mountain hurried Ningabiun.

At the break of day they each appeared at the great level on the mountain-top, Manabozho with twenty loads, at least, of the black stone, on one side, and on the other the West, with a whole meadow of bulrush in his arms.

Manabozho was the first to strike—hurling a great piece of the black rock, which struck the West directly between the eyes. The West returned the favor with a blow of bulrush that rung over the shoulders of Manabozho, far and wide, like the whip-thong of the lightning among the clouds.

And now both rallied, and Manabozho poured in a tempest of black rock, while Ningabiun discharged a shower of bulrush. Blow upon blow, thwack upon thwack—they fought hand to hand until black rock and

bulrush were all gone. Then they betook themselves
to hurling crags at each other, cudgeling with huge oak-
trees, and defying each other from one mountain-top
to another. At times they shot enormous boulders
of granite across at each other's heads, as though they
had been mere jack-stones. The battle, which had
commenced on the mountains, had extended far west.
The West was forced to give ground. Manabozho
pressing on, drove him across rivers and mountains,
ridges and lakes, till at last he got him to the very brink
of the world.

"Hold!" cried the West. "My son, you know my
power, and although I allow that I am now fairly
out of breath, it is impossible to kill me. Stop where
you are, and I will also portion you out with as much
power as your brothers. The four quarters of the
globe are already occupied, but you can go and do a
great deal of good to the people of the earth. They
are beset with serpents, beasts and monsters, who
make great havoc of human life. Go and do good, and
if you put forth half the strength you have to-day, you
will acquire a name that will last forever. When you
have finished your work I will have a place provided
for you. You will then go and sit with your brother,
Kabinocca, in the North."

Manabozho gave his father his hand upon this agreement. And parting from him, he returned to his own
grounds, where he lay for some time sore of his wounds.

These being, however, greatly allayed and soon after

cured by his grandmother's skill in medicines, Manabozho, as big and sturdy as ever, was ripe for new adventures. He set his thoughts immediately upon a war excursion against the Pearl Feather, a wicked old manito, who had killed his grandfather. Pearl Feather lived on the other side of the great lake, but that was nothing to Manabozho. He began his preparations by making huge bows and arrows without number; but he had no heads for his shafts. At last Noko told him that an old man, whom she knew, could furnish him with such as he needed. He sent her to get some. She soon returned with her wrapper full. Manabozho told her that he had not enough and sent her again. She came back with as many more. He thought to himself, "I must find out the way of making these heads."

Instead of directly asking how it was done, he preferred—it was just like Manabozho—to deceive his grandmother and come at the knowledge he desired by a trick.

"Noko," said he, "while I take my drum and rattle, and sing my war-songs, do you go and try to get me some larger heads, for these you have brought me are all of the same size. Go and see whether the old man is not willing to make some a little larger."

As she went he followed at a distance, having left his drum at the lodge, with a great bird tied at the top, whose fluttering should keep up the drum-beat the same as if he were tarrying at home. He saw the old

workman busy and learned how he prepared the heads;
he also beheld the old man's daughter, who was very
beautiful. Manabozho now discovered for the first
time that he had a heart of his own, and the sigh he
heaved passed through the arrow-maker's lodge like
a gale of wind.

"How it blows!" said the old man.

"It must be from the south," said the daughter;
"for it is very fragrant."

Manabozho slipped away, and in two strides he was
at home, shouting forth his songs as though he had
never left the lodge. He had just time to free the bird
which had been beating the drum, when his grandmother came in and delivered to him the big arrow-
heads.

In the evening the grandmother said, "My son, you
ought to fast before you go to war, as your brothers
do, to find out whether you will be successful or not."

He said he had no objection; and privately stored
away, in a shady place in the forest two or three dozen
juicy bears, a moose, and twenty strings of the tenderest birds. The place of his fast had been chosen by
Noko, and she had told him it must be so far as to be
beyond the sound of her voice or it would be unlucky.
So Manabozho would retire from the lodge so far as
to be entirely out of view of his grandmother, fall to
and enjoy himself heartily, and at nightfall, having
just despatched a dozen birds and half a bear or so,
he would return tottering and woe-begone, as if quite

famished, so as to move deeply the sympathies of his wise old granddame.

But after a time Manabozho, who was always spying out mischief, said to himself, "I must find out why my grandmother is so anxious to have me fast at this spot."

The next day he went but a short distance. She cried out, "A little farther off"; but he came nearer to the lodge, the rogue that he was, and cried out in a low, counterfeited voice, to make it appear that he was going away instead of approaching. He had now got so near that he could see all that passed in the lodge.

He had not been long in ambush when an old magician crept into the lodge. This old magician had very long hair, which hung across his shoulders and down his back like a bush or foot-mat. Noko welcomed him kindly and they commenced talking earnestly. In doing so, they put their two old heads so very close together that Manabozho was satisfied they were kissing each other. He was indignant that any one should take such a liberty with his venerable grandmother, and to mark his sense of the outrage, he touched the bushy hair of the old magician with a live coal which he had blown upon. The old magician felt the flame; he jumped out into the air, making his hair burn only the fiercer, and ran, blazing like a fire-ball, across the prairie.

Manabozho who had, meanwhile, stolen off to his

fasting-place, cried out in a heart-broken tone and as if on the very point of starvation, "Noko! Noko! is it time for me to come home?"

"Yes," she cried. And when he came in she asked him, "Did you see anything?"

"Nothing," he answered, with an air of childish candor; looking as much like a big simpleton as he could. The grandmother looked at him very closely and said no more.

Manabozho finished his term of fasting, in the course of which he slyly despatched twenty fat bears, six dozen birds, and two fine moose. Then he sang his war-song and embarked in his canoe, fully prepared for war. Besides weapons of battle, he had stowed in a large supply of oil.

He traveled rapidly night and day, for he had only to will or speak, and the canoe went. At length he arrived at a place guarded by many fiery serpents. He paused to view them, observing that they were some distance apart, and that the flames which they constantly belched forth reached across the pass. He gave them a good morning and began talking with them in a very friendly way; but they answered:

"We know you, Manabozho; you cannot pass."

He was not, however, to be put off so easily. Turning his canoe as if about to go back, he suddenly cried out with a loud and terrified voice:

"What is that behind you?"

The serpents, thrown off their guard, instantly

turned their heads, and he glided past them in a moment.

"Well," said he quietly, after he had got by, "how do you like my movement?"

He then took up his bow and arrows, and with deliberate aim shot every one of them, easily, for the serpents were fixed to one spot and could not even turn around. They were of an enormous length, and a bright color.

Having thus escaped the sentinel serpents, Manabozho pushed on in his canoe until he came to a part of the lake called Pitch-water, as whatever touched it was sure to stick fast. But Manabozho was prepared with his oil, and rubbing his canoe freely from end to end, he slipped through with ease, the first person who had ever succeeded in passing through the Pitch-water.

"There is nothing like a little oil to help one through pitch-water," said Manabozho to himself.

Now in view of land, he could see the lodge of Pearl Feather, the Shining Manito, high upon a distant hill.

Putting his clubs and arrows in order, Manabozho began his attack, yelling and shouting, beating his drum, and calling out in triple voices:

"Surround him! surround him! run up! run up!" making it appear that he had many followers. He advanced, shouting aloud:

"It was you that killed my grandfather," and shot off a whole forest of arrows.

The Pearl Feather appeared on the height, blazing like the sun, and paid back the discharges of Manabozho with a tempest of bolts, which rattled like the hail.

All day long the fight was kept up, and Manabozho had fired all of his arrows but three, without effect; for the Shining Manito was clothed in pure wampum. It was only by immense leaps to right and left that Manabozho could save his head from the sturdy blows which fell about him on every side, like pine-trees, from the hands of the Manito. He was badly bruised and at his very wits' end, when a large woodpecker flew past and lit on a tree. It was a bird he had known on the prairie, near his grandmother's lodge.

"Manabozho," called out the woodpecker, "your enemy has a weak point; shoot at the lock of hair on the crown of his head."

He shot his first arrow and only drew blood in a few drops. The Manito made one or two unsteady steps, then recovered himself. He began to parley, but Manabozho, knowing that he had discovered a way to reach him, was in no humor to trifle, and let slip another arrow, which brought the Shining Manito to his knees. And now, having the crown of his head within good range, Manabozho sent in his third arrow, which laid the Manito out upon the ground, stark dead.

Manabozho lifted up a huge war-cry, beat his drum, and took the scalp of the Manito as his trophy. Then calling the woodpecker to come and receive a reward for the timely hint he had given him, he rubbed the blood of the Shining Manito on the woodpecker's head, the feathers of which are red to this day. Full of his victory, Manabozho returned home, beating his war-drum furiously and shouting aloud his songs of triumph. His grandmother was on the shore ready to welcome him with the war-dance, which she performed with wonderful skill for one so far advanced in years.

The heart of Manabozho swelled within him. He was fairly on fire and an unconquerable desire for further adventures seized upon him. He had destroyed the powerful Pearl Feather, killed his serpents, and escaped all his wiles and charms. He had prevailed in a great land fight, his next trophy should be from the water.

He tried his prowess as a fisherman, and with such success that he captured a fish monstrous in size and so rich in fat that with the oil Manabozho was able to form a small lake. To this, being generously disposed and having a cunning purpose of his own to answer, he invited all the birds and beasts of his acquaintance; and he made the order in which they partook of the banquet the measure of their fatness for all time to come. As fast as they arrived he told them to plunge in and help themselves.

The first to make his appearance was the bear, who took a long and steady draught; then came the deer, the opossum, and such others of the family as are noted

for their comfortable case. The moose and bison were
slack in their cups, and the partridge, always lean in
flesh, looked on till the supply was nearly gone. There
was not a drop left by the time the hare and the mar-
tin appeared on the shore of the lake, and they are,
in consequence, the slenderest of all creatures.

When this ceremony was over, Manabozho suggested
to his friends, the assembled birds and animals, that
the occasion was proper for a little merry-making; and
taking up his drum, he cried out:

"New songs from the South! Come, brothers,
dance!"

In order to make the sport more mirthful, he directed that they should shut their eyes and pass
around him in a circle. Again he beat his drum and
cried out:

"New songs from the South! Come, brothers,
dance!"

They all fell in and commenced their rounds. Whenever Manabozho, as he stood in the circle, saw pass by
him a fat fowl which he fancied, he adroitly wrung
its neck and slipped it in his girdle, at the same time
beating his drum and singing at the top of his lungs
to drown the noise of the fluttering. And he all the
time called out in tones of admiration:

"That's the way, my brothers; that's the way!"

At last a small duck, of the diver family, thinking
there was something wrong, opened one eye and saw
what Manabozho was doing.

"Ha-ha-a! Manabozho is killing us!" he cried, giving a spring and making for the water.

Manabozho, quite vexed that the creature should have played the spy upon his house-keeping, followed him; and just as the duck was diving into the water, he gave him a kick, which is the reason that the diver's tail-feathers are few, his back flattened, and his legs straightened out, so that when he gets on land he makes a poor figure in walking.

Meantime, the other birds, having no ambition to be thrust in Manabozho's girdle, flew off, and the animals scampered into the woods.

Manabozho, stretching himself at ease in the shade along the side of the prairie, thought what he should do next. He concluded that he would travel and see new countries; and having once made up his mind, such was his length of limb and the immensity of his stride, that in less than three days he had walked over the entire continent and looked into every lodge by the way —and with such nicety of observation that he was able to inform his good old grandmother what each family had for a dinner at a given hour.

By way of relief to these grand doings, Manabozho was disposed to vary his experiences by bestowing a little time upon the sports of the woods. He had heard reported great feats in hunting, and he had a desire to try his power in that way. Besides that, it was a slight consideration that he had devoured all the game within reach of the lodge. And so, one evening, while walking along the shore of the great lake, weary and hungry, he was quite delighted to encounter a great magician in the form of an old wolf, with six young ones.

The wolf no sooner caught sight of him than he told his whelps, who were close about his side, to keep out of the way of Manabozho. "For I know," he said, "that it is that mischievous fellow whom we see yonder."

The young wolves were in the act of running off, when Manabozho cried out:

"My grandchildren, where are you going? Stop and I will go with you. I wish to have a little chat with your excellent father."

Saying which he advanced and greeted the old wolf, expressing himself pleased at seeing him looking so well.

"Whither do you journey?" he asked.

"We are looking for a good hunting-ground to pass the winter," the old wolf answered. "What brings you here?"

"I was looking for you," said Manabozho. "For I have a passion for the chase, brother. I always admired your family; are you willing to change me into a wolf?"

The wolf gave him a favorable answer, and he was forthwith changed into a wolf.

"Well, that will do," said Manabozho; then looking at his tail, he added, "Oh! could you oblige me by making my tail just a little longer and more bushy, please?"

"Certainly," said the old wolf; and he gave Manabozho such a length and spread of tail that it was constantly getting between his legs, and it was so heavy that it was as much as he could do to find strength to carry it. But having asked for it, he was ashamed to say a word; and they all started off in company, dashing up a ravine.

After getting into the woods for some distance, they fell in with the tracks of moose. The young ones scampered off in pursuit, the old wolf and Manabozho following at their leisure.

"Well," said the old wolf, by way of opening discourse, "who do you think is the fastest of the boys? Can you tell by the jumps they take?"

"Why," Manabozho replied, "that one that takes such long jumps, he is the fastest, to be sure!"

"Ha! ha! you are mistaken," said the old wolf. "He makes a good start, but he will be the first to tire out; this one, who appears to be behind, will be the one to kill the game."

By this time they had come to the spot where the boys had started in chase. One had dropped what seemed to be a small medicine-sack, which he carried for the use of the hunting-party.

"Take that, Manabozho," said the old wolf.

"Esa," he replied, "what will I do with a dirty dog-skin?"

The old wolf took it up; it was a beautiful robe.

"Oh, I will carry it now," cried Manabozho.

"Oh, no," said the old wolf, who had exerted his magical powers, "it is a robe of pearls. Come along!"

And away sped the old wolf at a great rate of speed.

"Not so fast," called Manabozho after him; and then he added to himself as he panted after, "Oh, this tail!"

Coming to a place where the moose had lain down, they saw that the young wolves had made a fresh start after their prey.

"Why," said the old wolf, "this moose is poor. I know by the tracks; in that way I can always tell whether they are fat or not."

A little farther on, one of the young wolves, in dashing at the moose, had broken a tooth on a tree.

"Manabozho," said the old wolf, "one of your grandchildren has shot at the game. Take his arrow; there it is."

"No," replied Manabozho; "what will I do with a dirty dog's tooth?"

The old wolf took it up, and behold it was a beautiful silver arrow.

When they at last overtook them, they found that the youngsters had killed a very fat moose. Manabozho was exceedingly hungry; but the old wolf just then again exerted his magical powers, and Manabozho saw nothing but the bones picked quite clean. He thought to himself, "Just as I expected! Dirty, greedy fellows! If it had not been for this log at my back, I should have been in time to have got a mouthful"; and he cursed the bushy tail which he carried, to the bottom of his heart. He, however, sat down without saying a word.

At length the old wolf spoke to one of the young ones, saying:

"Give some meat to your grandfather."

One of them obeyed, and coming near to Manabozho, he presented him the other end of his own bushy tail, which was nicely seasoned with burrs gathered in the course of the hunt.

Manabozho jumped up and called out:

"You dog, now that your stomach is full, do you think I am going to eat you to get at my dinner? Get you gone into some other place."

Saying which, Manabozho, in his anger, walked off by himself.

"Come back, brother," cried the wolf. "You are losing your eyes."

Manabozho turned back.

"You do the child injustice. Look there!" and behold, a heap of fresh, ruddy meat was lying on the spot, already prepared.

Manabozho, at the view of so much good provision, put on a smiling face.

"Amazement!" he said; "how fine the meat is!"

"Yes," replied the old wolf, "it is always so with

us; we know our work and always get the best. It is not a long tail that makes the hunter."

Manabozho bit his lip.

They now fixed their winter quarters. The youngsters went out in search of game, and they soon brought in a large supply. One day, during the absence of the young hunters, the old wolf amused himself in cracking the large bones of a moose.

"Manabozho," said he, "cover your head with the robe, and do not look at me while I am busy with these bones, for a piece may fly in your eye."

Manabozho did as he was bid; but looking through a rent in the robe, he saw what the other was about. Just at that moment a piece flew off and hit him on the eye. He cried out:

"Tyau, why do you strike me, you old dog?"

The wolf answered—"You must have been looking at me."

"No, no," retorted Manabozho, "why should I want to look at you?"

"Manabozho," said the old wolf, "you must have been looking or you would not have got hurt."

"No, no," he replied again, "I was not." But he thought to himself, "I will repay the saucy wolf this mischief."

So the next day, taking up a bone to obtain the marrow, he said to the wolf:

"Brother, cover your head and do not look at me, for I very much fear a piece may fly in your eye."

The wolf did so; and Manabozho, taking the large leg-bone of the moose, first looking to see if the wolf was well covered, hit him a blow with all his might. The wolf jumped up, cried out, and fell prostrate from the effects of the blow.

"Why," said he, when he came to a little and was able to sit up, "why did you strike me so?"

"Strike you?" said Manabozho, with well-feigned surprise. "No; you must have been looking at me."

"No," answered the wolf, "I say I have not."

But Manabozho insisted, and as the old wolf was no great master of tricky argument, he was obliged to give it up.

Shortly after this the old wolf suggested to Manabozho that he should go out and try his luck in hunting by himself.

When he chose to put his mind upon it Manabozho was quite expert, and this time he succeeded in killing a fine fat moose, which he thought he would take aside slyly and devour alone, having prepared to tell the old wolf a pretty story on his return, to account for his failure to bring anything with him.

He was very hungry, and he sat down to eat; but as he never could go to work in a straightforward way, he immediately fell into great doubts as to the proper point at which to begin.

"Well," said he, "I do not know where to commence. At the head? No. People will laugh, and say—'He ate him backward.'"

He went to the side. "No," said he, "they will say I ate him sideways."

He then went to the hind-quarter. "No, that will not do, either; they will say I ate him forward. I will begin here, say what they will."

He took a delicate piece from the small of the back and was just on the point of putting it to his mouth, when a tree close by made a creaking noise. He seemed vexed at the sound. He raised the morsel to his mouth the second time, when the tree creaked again.

"Why," he exclaimed, "I cannot eat when I hear such a noise. Stop, stop!" he said to the tree. He put the meat down, exclaiming—"I cannot eat with such a noise"; and starting away he climbed the tree, and was pulling at the limb which had offended him, when his fore-paw was caught between the branches so that he could not free himself.

While thus held fast, he saw a pack of wolves advancing through the wood in the direction of his meat. He suspected them to be the old wolf and his cubs, but night was coming on and he could not make them out.

"Go the other way, go the other way!" he cried out; "what would you come to get here?"

The wolves stopped for a while and talked among themselves, and said:

"Manabozho must have something there, or he would not tell us to go another way."

"I begin to know him," said the old wolf, "and all his tricks. Let us go forward and see."

They came on, and finding the moose, they soon made away with it. Manabozho looked wistfully on to see them eat till they were fully satisfied, when they scampered off in high spirits.

A heavy blast of wind opened the branches and released Manabozho, who found that the wolves had left nothing but the bare bones. He made for home, where, when he related his mishap, the old wolf took him by the fore-paw and condoled with him deeply on his ill-luck. A tear even started to his eye as he said:

"My brother, this should teach us not to meddle with points of ceremony when we have good meat to eat."

On a bright morning in the early spring, the winter having by this time drawn fairly to a close, the old wolf addressed Manabozho:

"My brother, I am obliged to leave you; and although I have sometimes been merry at your expense, I will show that I care for your comfort. I shall leave one of the boys behind me to be your hunter and to keep you company through the long summer afternoons."

The old wolf galloped off with his five young ones; and as they disappeared from view, Manabozho was disenchanted in a moment and returned to his mortal shape.

Although he had been sometimes vexed and im-

posed upon, he had, altogether, passed a pleasant winter with the cunning old wolf, and now that he was
gone, Manabozho was downcast and low in spirit. But
as the days grew brighter he recovered by degrees his
air of cheerful confidence and was ready to try his
hand upon any new adventure that might occur to
him. The old spirit of mischief was still alive within
him.

The young wolf who had been left with him was a
good hunter and never failed to keep the lodge well
supplied with meat. One day Manabozho addressed
him as follows:

"My grandson, I had a dream last night, and it does
not portend good. It is of the large lake which lies
in that direction. You must be careful always to go
across it, whether the ice seem strong or not. Never
go around it, for there are enemies on the further
shore who lie in wait for you. The ice is always safe."

Now Manabozho knew well that the ice was thin-
ning every day under the warm sun, but he could not
stay himself from playing a trick upon the young
wolf.

In the evening when he came to the lake, after a
long day's travel in quest of game, the young wolf,
confiding to his grandfather, said, "Hwooh! the ice
does look thin, but Nesho says it is sound"; and he
trotted upon the glassy plain.

He had not got half way across when the ice snapped,
and with a mournful cry, the young wolf fell in and

was immediately seized by the water-serpents. They knew that it was Manabozho's grandson and were thirsting for revenge upon him for the death of their relations in the war upon Pearl Feather.

Manabozho heard the young wolf's cry as he sat in his lodge; he knew what had happened; and from that moment he was deprived of the greater part of his magical power.

He returned scarcely more than an ordinary mortal to his former place of dwelling, whence his grandmother had departed no one knew whither. He married the arrow-maker's daughter, and became the father of several children, and very poor. He was scarcely able to procure the means of living. His lodge was pitched in a remote part of the country where he could get no game. It was winter, and he had not the common comforts of life.

He said to his wife one day:

"I will go out a-walking and see if I can not find some lodges."

After walking some time he saw a lodge at a distance. The children were playing at the door. When they saw him approaching they ran in and told their parents that Manabozho was coming.

It was the residence of the large red-headed woodpecker. He came to the door and asked Manabozho to enter. This invitation was promptly accepted.

After some time, the woodpecker, who was a magician, said to his wife:

"Have you nothing to give Manabozho? He must be hungry."

She answered, "No."

"He ought not to go without his supper," said the woodpecker. "I will see what I can do."

In the center of the lodge stood a large tamarack tree. Upon this the woodpecker flew, and commenced going up, turning his head on each side of the tree and every now and then driving in his bill. At last he pulled something out of the tree and threw it down; when, behold! a fine fat raccoon lay on the ground. He drew out six or seven more. He then descended and told his wife to prepare them.

"Manabozho," he said, "this is the only thing we eat; what else can we give you?"

"It is very good," replied Manabozho.

They smoked their pipes and conversed with each other.

After eating, Manabozho got ready to go home. Then the woodpecker said to his wife, "Give him the other raccoons to take home for his children."

In the act of leaving the lodge, Manabozho, on purpose, dropped one of his mittens, which was soon after observed upon the ground.

"Run," said the woodpecker to his eldest son, "and give it to him; but mind that you do not give it into his hand; throw it at him, for there is no knowing him, he acts so curiously."

The boy did as he was directed.

"Grandfather," said he to Manabozho, as he came up to him, "you have left one of your mittens. Here it is."

"Yes," he said, affecting to be ignorant of the circumstance, "it is so; but don't throw it, you will soil it on the snow."

The lad, however, threw it, and was about to return, when Manabozho cried out:

"Bakah! Bakah! stop—stop! Is that all you eat? Do you eat nothing else with your raccoon? Tell me!"

"Yes, that is all," answered the young Woodpecker; "we have nothing else."

"Tell your father," continued Manabozho, "to come and visit me, and let him bring a sack. I will give him what he shall eat with his raccoon-meat."

When the young one returned and reported this message to his father, the old woodpecker turned up his nose at the invitation.

"I wonder," he said, "what he thinks he has got, poor fellow!"

He was bound, however, to answer the proffer of hospitality, so he went accordingly to pay a visit to Manabozho, taking along a cedar-sack.

Manabozho received the old red-headed woodpecker with great ceremony. He had stood at the door awaiting his arrival, and as soon as he came in sight Manabozho commenced, while he was yet far off, bowing and opening wide his arms in token of welcome; all of which the woodpecker returned in due form by ducking his bill and hopping to right and left upon the ground, extending his wings to their full length and fluttering them back to his breast.

When the woodpecker at last reached the lodge, Manabozho made various remarks upon the weather, the appearance of the country, and especially on the scarcity of game.

"But we," he added, "we always have enough. Come in, and you shall not go away hungry, my noble bird!"

Manabozho had always prided himself on being able to give as good as he had received; and to be up with the woodpecker, he had shifted his lodge so as to inclose a large dry tamarack tree.

"What can I give you?" said he to the woodpecker. "But as we eat so shall you eat."

With this Manabozho hopped forward, and jumping on the tamarack tree, attempted to climb it just as he had seen the woodpecker do in his own lodge. He turned his head first on one side, then on the other, in the manner of the bird, meanwhile striving to go up, and as often slipping down. Ever and anon he would strike the tree with his nose, as if it had been a bill, and draw back, but he pulled out no raccoons; and he dashed his nose so often against the trunk that at last the blood began to flow, and he tumbled down senseless upon the ground.

The woodpecker started up with his drum and rattle

and by beating them violently he succeeded in bringing him to.

As soon as he came to his senses, Manabozho began to lay the blame of his failure upon his wife, saying to his guest:

"Nemesho, it is this woman-relation of yours—she is the cause of my not succeeding. She has made me a worthless fellow. Before I took her I also could get raccoons."

The woodpecker said nothing, but flying on the tree, drew out several fine raccoons.

"Here," said he, "this is the way we do!" and left in disdain, carrying his bill high in the air and stepping over the door-sill as if it were not worthy to be touched by his toes.

After this visit, Manabozho was sitting in the lodge one day with his head down. He heard the wind whistling around it, and thought that by attentively listening he could hear the voice of some one speaking to him. It seemed to say to him:

"Great chief, why are you sorrowful? Am not I your friend—your guardian spirit?"

Manabozho immediately took up his rattle, and without rising from the ground where he was sitting, began to sing the chant which has at every close the refrain of, "Wha lay le aw."

When he had dwelt for a long time on this peculiar chant, which he had been used to sing in all his times

of trouble, he laid his rattle aside and determined to
fast. For this purpose he went to a cave which faced
the setting sun and built a very small fire, near which
he lay down, first telling his wife that neither she nor
the children must come near him till he had finished his
fast.

At the end of seven days he came back to the lodge,
pale and thin, looking like a spirit himself, and as if he
had seen spirits. His wife had in the meantime dug
through the snow and got a few of the roots called
truffles. These she boiled and set before him, and this
was all the food they had or seemed likely to obtain.

When he had finished his light repast, Manabozho
took up his station in the door to see what would
happen. As he stood thus, holding in his hand his
large bow, with a quiver well filled with arrows, a
deer glided past along the far edge of the prairie; but
it was miles away, and no shaft that Manabozho could
shoot would be able to touch it.

Presently a cry come down the air, and looking up
he beheld a great flight of birds; but they were so far
up in the sky that he would have lost his arrows in a
vain attempt among the clouds.

Still he stood watchful and confident that some turn
of luck was about to occur, when there came near to
the lodge two hunters, who bore between them on poles,
a bear; and it was so fine and fat a bear that it was as
much as the two hunters could do with all their strength
to carry it.

As they came to the lodge-door, one of the hunters asked if Manabozho lived thereabout.

"He is here," answered Manabozho.

"I have often heard of you," said the first hunter, "and I was curious to see you. But you have lost your magical power. Do you know whether any of it is left?"

Manabozho answered that he was himself in the dark on the subject.

"Suppose you make a trial," said the hunter.

"What shall I do?" asked Manabozho.

"There is my friend," said the hunter, pointing to his companion, "who with me owns this bear which we are carrying home. Suppose you see if you can change him into a piece of rock."

"Very well," said Manabozho; and he had scarcely spoken before the other hunter became a rock.

"Now change him back again," said the first hunter.

"That I can't do," Manabozho answered; "there my power ends."

The hunter looked at the rock with a bewildered face.

"What shall I do?" he asked. "This bear I can never carry alone, and it was agreed between my friend there and myself, that we should not divide it till we reached home. Can't you change my friend back, Manabozho?"

"I would like to oblige you," answered Manabozho, "but it is utterly out of my power."

With this, looking again at the rock with a sad and

bewildered face, and then casting a sorrowful glance at the bear, which lay by the door of the lodge, the hunter took his leave, bewailing bitterly at heart the loss of his friend and his bear.

He was scarcely out of sight when Manabozho sent the children to get red willow sticks. Of these he cut off as many pieces of equal length as would serve to invite his friends among the beasts and birds to a feast. A red stick was sent to each one, not forgetting the woodpecker and his family.

When they arrived they were astonished to see such an abundance of meat prepared for them at such a time of scarcity. Manabozho understood their glance and was proud of a chance to make such a display.

"Akewazi," he said to the oldest of the party, "the weather is very cold, and the snow lasts a long time; we can kill nothing now but small squirrels, and they are all black. I have sent for you to help me eat some of them."

The woodpecker was the first to try a mouthful of the bear's meat, but he had no sooner begun to taste it than it changed into a dry powder and set him coughing. It appeared as bitter as ashes.

The moose was affected in the same way, and it brought on such a dry cough as to shake every bone in his body.

One by one, each in turn joined the company of coughers, except Manabozho and his family, to whom the bear's meat proved very savory.

But the visitors had too high a sense of what was due to decorum and good manners to say anything. The meat looked very fine, and being keenly set and strongly tempted by its promising look, they thought they would try more of it. The more they ate the faster they coughed and the louder became the uproar, until Manabozho, exerting the magical gift which he found he retained, changed them all into squirrels; and to this day the squirrel suffers from the same dry cough which was brought on by attempting to sup off of Manabozho's ashen bear's meat.

And even after this transformation, when Manabozho lacked provisions for his family, he would hunt the squirrel, a supply of which never failed him, so that he was always sure to have a number of his friends present, in this shape, at the banquet.

The rock into which he changed the hunter, thus becoming possessed of the bear, and laying the foundations of his good fortune, ever after remained by his lodge-door, and it was called the Game-Bag of Manabozho, the Mischief-Maker.

III

THE CELESTIAL SISTERS

WAUPEE, or the White Hawk, lived in a remote part of the forest, where animals abounded. Every day he returned from the chase with a large spoil, for he was one of the most skilful and lucky hunters of his tribe. His form was like the cedar; the fire of youth beamed from his eye; there was no forest too gloomy for him to penetrate, and no track made by bird or beast of any kind which he could not readily follow.

One day he had gone beyond any point which he had ever before visited. He traveled through an open wood, which enabled him to see a great distance. At length he beheld a light breaking through the foliage of the distant trees, which made him sure that he was on the borders of a prairie. It was a wide plain, covered with long blue grass, and enamelled with flowers of a thousand lovely tints.

After walking for some time without a path, musing upon the open country and enjoying the fragrant breeze, he suddenly came to a ring worn among the grass and the flowers, as if it had been made by footsteps moving lightly round and round. But it was strange—so strange as to cause the White Hawk to

pause and gaze long and fixedly upon the ground—
there was no path which led to this flowery circle.
There was not even a crushed leaf or a broken twig,
nor did he find the least trace of a footstep, approaching or retiring. So wondering he thought he would
hide himself and lie in wait to discover, if he could,
what this strange circle meant.

Presently he heard faint sounds of music in the air.
Looking up in the direction they came from, he saw
floating a small object, like a little summer cloud that
approaches down from above the earth. At first it
was very small, and seemed as if it could have been
blown away by the first breeze that came along; but it
rapidly grew as he gazed upon it, and the music every
moment came clearer and more sweetly to his ear. As
it neared the earth it appeared as a basket, and it was
filled with twelve sisters, of the most lovely forms and
enchanting beauty.

As soon as the basket touched the ground they
leaped out, and began straightway to dance around
the magic ring, in the most joyous manner, striking a
shining ball, which uttered ravishing melodies, keeping
time as they danced.

The White Hawk, from his concealment, gazed with
delight upon their graceful forms and movements. He
admired them all, but he was most pleased with the
youngest. He longed to be at her side, to embrace
her, to call her his own; and unable to remain longer a
silent admirer, he rushed out and endeavored to seize

this twelfth beauty who so enchanted him. But the sisters, the moment they descried the form of a man, leaped back into the basket with the swiftness of birds, and were drawn up into the sky.

Lamenting his ill-luck, Waupee gazed longingly upon the fairy basket as it ascended bearing the lovely sisters from his view.

"They are gone," he said, "and I shall see them no more."

He returned to his solitary lodge, but found no relief to his mind. He walked abroad, but to look at the sky, which had withdrawn from his sight the only being he had ever loved, was painful to him now.

The next day, selecting the same hour, the White Hawk went back to the prairie, and took his station near the ring. But in order to deceive the sisters, he assumed the form of an opossum, and sat among the grass as if he were there engaged in chewing the cud. He had not waited long when he saw the cloudy basket descend, and heard the same sweet music falling as before. He crept slowly toward the ring; but the instant the sisters caught sight of him they were startled, and sprang into their car. It rose a short distance when one of the elder sisters spoke:

"Perhaps," she said, "it has come to show us how the game is played by mortals."

"Oh, no," the youngest replied; "quick, let us ascend."

And all joining in a chant, they rose out of sight.

Then Waupee, casting off his disguise, walked sorrowfully back to his lodge—but ah, the night seemed very long to lonely White Hawk! His whole soul was filled with the thought of the beautiful sister.

Betimes, the next day, he returned to the haunted spot, hoping and fearing, and sighing as though his very soul would leave his body in its anguish. He reflected upon the plan he should follow to secure success. He had already failed twice; to fail a third time would be fatal. By searching he found nearby an old stump, much covered with moss, and just then in use as the residence of a number of mice, who had stopped there on a pilgrimage to some relatives on the other side of the prairie. The White Hawk was so pleased with their tidy little forms that he thought he, too, would be a mouse, especially as they were by no means formidable to look at, and would not be at all likely to create alarm.

He accordingly brought the stump and set it near the ring. Then, without further notice, he became a mouse, and peeped and sported, and kept his sharp little eyes busy with the others; only he did not forget to keep one eye up toward the sky, and one ear wide open in the same direction.

It was not long before the sisters, at their customary hour, came down and resumed their sport.

"But see," cried the youngest sister, "that stump was not there before."

She ran off, frightened, toward the basket. But her

sisters only smiled, and gathering round the old tree-stump, struck it, in jest, when out ran the mice, and among them Waupee. This was sport for the sisters and they chased and killed them all save one, which was pursued by the twelfth sister, who had decided after all to join in the game. As she raised a silver stick which she held in her hand to put an end to that, too, the form of the White Hawk arose, and he clasped his prize in his arms. The other eleven sprang to their basket, and were drawn up to the skies.

Delighted with his success, Waupee exerted all his skill to please his bride and win her affections. He wiped the tears from her eyes; he related his adventures in the chase; he dwelt upon the charms of life on the earth. He was constant in his attentions, keeping fondly by her side, and picking out the way for her to walk as he led her gently toward his lodge. He felt his heart glow with joy as he entered it, and from that moment he was one of the happiest of men.

Winter and summer passed rapidly away, and as spring drew near with its balmy gales and its many-colored flowers, their happiness was increased by the presence of a beautiful boy in their lodge, a son with both his mother's beauty and his father's strength. What more of earthly blessing was there for them to enjoy?

Waupee's wife, however, was a daughter of one of the stars; and as the scenes of earth began to pall upon her sight, she sighed to revisit her father. But she hid these feelings from her husband. She remembered the charm that would carry her up, and while White Hawk was engaged in the chase, she took occasion to construct a wicker basket, which she kept concealed. In the meantime, she collected such rarities from the earth as she thought would please her father, as well as the most dainty kinds of food.

Then on a day when all was in readiness and Waupee absent, she went out to the charmed ring, taking with her her little son. As they entered the car she commenced her magical song, and the basket rose. The song was sad, and of a lowly and mournful cadence, and as it was wafted far away by the wind, it caught her husband's ear. It was a voice which he well knew, and he instantly ran to the prairie. But though he made breathless speed, he could not reach the ring before his wife and child had ascended beyond his reach. He lifted up his voice in loud appeals, but they were unavailing. The basket still went up. He watched it till it became a small speck, and finally it vanished in the sky. He then bent his head down to the ground and was miserable.

Through a long winter and a long summer Waupee bewailed his loss, but he found no relief. The beautiful spirit had come and gone, and he should see it no more!

In the meantime his wife had reached her home in the stars, and in the blissful employments of her father's house she almost forgot that she had left a husband upon the earth. But her son, as he grew up, resembled his father more and more, and every day he was restless and anxious to revisit the scene of his birth. His grandfather, perceiving this, said to his daughter:

"Go, my child, take your son down to his father, and ask him to come up and live with us. But tell him to bring along a specimen of each kind of bird and animal he kills in the chase."

The mother accordingly took the boy and descended. And the White Hawk, who was ever near the enchanted spot, heard her voice as she came down the sky. His heart beat with impatience as he saw her form and that of his son, and they were soon clasped in his arms.

He heard the message of the Star, and he began to hunt with the greatest activity, that he might collect the present with all despatch. He spent whole nights, as well as days, in searching for every curious and beautiful animal and bird. But he only preserved a foot, a wing, or a tail of each.

When all was ready, Waupee visited once more each favorite spot—the hill-top whence he had been used to see the rising sun; the stream where he had sported as a boy; the old lodge, which he was to sit in no more; and last of all, he came to the magic circle, and gazed widely around him with tearful eyes. Then taking his wife and child by the hand, he entered the car, and they were drawn up—into a country far beyond the flight of birds, or the power of mortal eye to pierce.

Great joy was manifested upon their arrival at the starry plains. The Star Chief invited all his people to a feast; and when they had assembled, he proclaimed aloud that each one might continue as he was, an inhabitant of his own dominions, or select of the earthly gifts such as he liked best. A very strange confusion immediately arose; not one but sprang forward. Some chose a foot, some a wing, some a tail, and some a claw. Those who selected tails or claws were changed into animals and ran off; the others assumed the form of birds and flew away. Waupee chose a white hawk's feather. His wife and son followed his example, and each one became a white hawk. He spread his wings, and, followed by his wife and son, descended with the other birds to the earth, where they are still to be found, with the brightness of the starry plains in their eyes and the freedom of the heavenly breezes in their wings.

IV

GRAY EAGLE AND HIS FIVE BROTHERS

THERE were six falcons living in a nest, five of whom were still too young to fly, when it so happened that both the parent birds were shot in one day. The young brood waited anxiously for their return; but night came, and they were left without parents and without food.

Gray Eagle, the eldest, and the only one whose feathers had become stout enough to enable him to leave the nest, took his place at the head of the family and assumed the duty of stifling his brothers' cries and providing the little household with food. In this he was very successful. But one day, while out on a foraging excursion, he got one of his wings broken. This was more to be regretted as the season had arrived when they were soon to go to a southern country to pass the winter, and the children were only waiting to become a little stronger and more expert on the wing to set out on the journey.

Finding that their elder brother did not return, they resolved to go in search of him. After beating up and down the country for the better part of a whole day, they at last found him, sorely wounded and unable to fly, lodged in the upper branches of a sycamore tree.

"Brothers," said Gray Eagle, as they gathered around, questioning him about his injuries, "an accident has befallen me, but let not this prevent your going to a warmer climate. Winter is rapidly approaching, and you cannot remain here. It is better that I alone should die, than for you all to suffer on my account."

"No, no," they replied, with one voice. "We will not forsake you. We will share your sufferings; we will abandon our journey and take care of you as you did of us before we were able to take care of ourselves. If the chill climate kills you, it shall kill us. Do you think we can so soon forget your brotherly care, which has equalled a father's, and even a mother's kindness? Whether you live or die, we will live or die with you."

They sought out a hollow tree to winter in, and contrived to carry their wounded nest-mate thither; and before the rigor of the season had set in, they had, by diligence and economy, stored up food enough to carry them through the winter months.

To make the provisions they had laid in last the better, it was agreed among them that two of their number should go south, leaving the other three to watch over, feed, and protect their wounded brother. So the travelers set forth, sorry to leave home, but resolved that the first promise of spring should bring them back again. And the three who remained, mounting to the very peak of the tree and bearing Gray Eagle in their arms, watched them, as they vanished away southward, till their forms blended with the air and were wholly lost to sight.

Then Gray Eagle was propped up in a snug fork with cushions of dry moss, and the household was set in order. The oldest of the five younger brothers took upon himself the charge of nursing Gray Eagle, preparing his food, bringing him water, and changing his pillows when he grew tired of one position. He also looked to it that the house itself was kept in a tidy condition, and that the pantry was supplied with food. To the next brother was assigned the duty of physician, and he was to prescribe such herbs and other medicines as the health of Gray Eagle seemed to require. As the doctor brother had no other invalid on his visiting-list, he devoted the time not given to the cure of his patient to the killing of game wherewith to stock the housekeeper's larder; so that, whatever he did, he was always busy in the line of professional duty—killing or curing. On his hunting excursions Doctor Falcon carried with him his youngest brother, who, being a foolish young fellow and inexperienced in the ways of the world, it was not thought safe to trust alone.

In due time, what with good nursing, good feeding, and good air, Gray Eagle recovered from his wound; and he then repaid the kindness of his brothers by giving them such advice and instruction in the art of hunting as his age and experience qualified him to impart. As spring advanced they began to look about for the means of replenishing their storehouse, whose supplies were running low; and they were all quite successful in their quest except the youngest, whose name was Peepi, or the Pigeon-Hawk. He had of late begun to set up for himself, but being small and foolish and feather-headed, flying hither and yonder without any set purpose, it so happened that Peepi always came home, so to phrase it, with an empty game-bag and his pinions terribly rumpled.

At last Gray Eagle spoke to him and demanded the cause of his ill-luck.

"It is not my smallness or weakness of body," Peepi answered, "that prevents my bringing home provender as well as my brothers. I am all the time on the wing, hither and thither. I kill ducks and other birds every time I go out; but just as I get to the woods, on my way home, I am met by a large ko-ko-ho, who robs me of my prey; and," added Peepi, with great energy, "it's my settled opinion that the villain lies in wait for the very purpose of doing so."

"I have no doubt you are right, Brother Peepi," rejoined Gray Eagle. "I know this pirate—his name is White Owl; and now that I feel my strength fully recovered, I will go out with you to-morrow and help you look after this greedy bush-ranger."

The next day they went forth in company and arrived at a fine fresh-water lake. Gray Eagle seated himself hard by, while Peepi started out. The latter soon pounced upon a duck.

"Well done!" thought his brother, who saw his success; but just as little Peepi was getting to land with his prize, up sailed a large white owl from a tree where he, too, had been watching, and laid claim to it. He was on the point of wresting it from Peepi, when Gray Eagle, calling out to the intruder to stop, rushed up, fixed his talons in both sides of the owl, and without further introduction or ceremony flew away with him.

The little Pigeon-Hawk followed closely, with the duck under his wing, rejoiced and happy to think that he had something to carry home at last. He was naturally much vexed with the owl, and had no sooner delivered over the duck to the housekeeper, than he flew in the owl's face and, venting an abundance of reproaches, would have torn the very eyes out of the White Owl's head in his passion.

"Softly, Peepi," said the Gray Eagle, stepping in between them. "Don't be in such a huff, my little brother, or show so revengeful a temper. Do you not know that we are to forgive our enemies? White Owl, you may go; but let this be a lesson to you, not to play the tyrant over those who may chance to be weaker than yourself."

So, after adding to this much more good advice and telling him what kind of herbs would cure his wounds,

Gray Eagle dismissed White Owl, and the brothers sat down to supper.

The next day, betimes, before the household had fairly rubbed the cobwebs out of the corners of their eyes, there came a knock at the front door—which was a dry branch that lay down before the hollow of the tree in which they lodged—and being called to come in, who should make their appearance but the two nest-mates, who had just returned from the South where they had been wintering. There was great rejoicing over their return, and now that they were all happily reunited, each one soon chose a mate and began to keep house in the woods for himself.

Spring had now revisited the North. The cold winds had all blown themselves away, the ice had melted, the streams were open and smiled as they looked at the blue sky once more; and the forests, far and wide, in their green mantle, echoed every cheerful sound.

But it is in vain that spring returns, and that the heart of Nature is opened in bounty, if we are not thankful to the Master of Life, who has preserved us through the winter. Nor does that man answer the end for which he was made who does not show a kind and charitable feeling to all who are in want or sickness.

The love and harmony of Gray Eagle and his brothers continued. They never forgot each other. Every week, on the fourth afternoon of the week (for that was the time when they had found their wounded elder brother), they had a meeting in the hollow of the old sycamore tree, when they talked over family matters and advised with each other about their affairs, as brothers should.

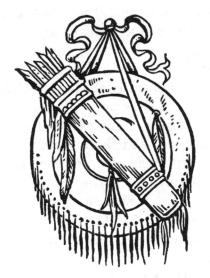

V

HE OF THE LITTLE SHELL

ONCE upon a time, all the people of a certain country had died, excepting two helpless children, a baby boy and a little girl.

When their parents died, these children were asleep. The little girl, who was the elder, was the first to awake. She looked around her, but seeing nobody but her little brother, who lay smiling in his dreams, she quietly resumed her bed.

At the end of ten days her brother moved, without opening his eyes.

At the end of ten days more he changed his position, lying on the other side, and in this way he kept on sleeping for a long time; and pleasant, too, must have been his dreams, for his little sister never looked at him that he was not quite a little heaven of smiles and flashing lights, which beamed about his head and filled the lodge with a strange splendor.

The girl soon grew to be a woman, but the boy increased in stature very slowly. It was a long time before he could even creep, and he was well advanced in years before he could stand alone. When he was able to walk, his sister made him a little bow and arrows, and hung around his neck a small shell, saying:

"You shall be called Dais-Imid, or He of the Little Shell."

Every day he would go out with his bow, shooting at the small birds. The first bird he killed was a tom-tit. His sister was highly pleased when he took it to her. She carefully prepared and stuffed it, and put it away for him.

The next day he killed a red squirrel. His sister preserved this, too. The third day he killed a partridge, and this they had for their evening meal.

After this he acquired more courage and would venture some distance from home. His skill and success daily increased, and he killed the deer, bear, moose, and other large animals inhabiting the forest.

At last, although so very small of stature, he became a great hunter, and all that he shot he brought home and shared with his sister; and whenever he entered the lodge, a light beamed about his head and filled the place with a strange splendor.

He had now arrived at the years of manhood, but he still remained a perfect infant in size.

One day, walking about in quest of game, he came to a small lake.

It was in the winter season; and upon the ice of the lake he saw a man of giant height, employed in killing beavers.

Comparing himself with this great man, he felt that

he was no bigger than an insect. He seated himself on the shore and watched his movements.

When the large man had killed many beavers, he put them on a hand-sled which he had, and pursued his way home. When he saw him retire, the dwarf hunter followed, and, wielding his magic shell, he cut off the tail of one of the beavers and ran home with the prize.

The giant, on reaching his lodge with his sled-load of beavers, was surprised to find one of them shorn of its tail.

The next day the little hero of the shell went to the same lake. The giant, who had been busy there for some time, had already loaded his sled and commenced his return; but running nimbly forward and overtaking him, Dais-Imid succeeded in securing another of the beaver-tails.

"I wonder," said the giant, on reaching his lodge and overlooking his beavers, "what dog it is that has thus cheated me. Could I meet him, I would make his flesh quiver at the point of my javelin."

The giant forgot that he had taken without permission these very beavers out of a beaver-dam which belonged to the little shell-man and his sister.

The next day he pursued his hunting at the beaver-dam near the lake, and he was again followed by the little man with the shell.

This time the giant was so nimble in his movements that he had nearly reached home before Little Shell could overtake him; but making his best speed, he was just in time to clip another beaver's tail before the sled slipped into the lodge.

The giant would have been a patient giant, indeed, if his anger had not been violent at these constant tricks played upon him. What vexed him most, was, that he could not get sight of his enemy. Sharp eyes he would have needed to do so, inasmuch as He of the Little Shell had the gift of making himself invisible whenever he chose.

The giant, giving vent to his feelings with many loud rumbling words, looked sharply around to see whether he could discover any tracks. He could find none. The unknown had stepped too lightly to leave the slightest mark behind.

The next day the giant resolved to disappoint his mysterious follower by going to the beaver-dam very early; and accordingly, when Dais-Imid came to the place, he found the fresh traces of his work, but the giant had already gone away. He followed hard upon his tracks but failed to overtake him. When He of the Little Shell came in sight of the lodge, the stranger was in front of it, employed in skinning his beavers.

As Dais-Imid stood looking at him—he had been all this time invisible—he thought:

"I will let him have a view of me."

Presently the man, who proved to be no less a personage than the celebrated giant, Manabozho, looked up and saw him. After regarding him with attention, he said:

"Who are you, little man? I have a mind to kill you."

The little hero of the shell replied:

"If you were to try to kill me you could not do it."

With this speech of the little man, Manabozho grabbed at him; but when he thought to have had him in his hand, Little Shell was gone.

"Where are you now, little man?" cried Manabozho.

"Here, under your girdle," answered the shell-dwarf. At which giant Manabozho, thinking to crush him, slapped down his great hand with all his might; but on unloosing his girdle he was disappointed at finding no dwarf there.

"Where are you now, little man?" he cried again, in a greater rage than ever.

"In your right nostril!" the dwarf replied. Whereupon the giant Manabozho seized himself by the finger and thumb at the place, and gave it a violent tweak; but as he immediately heard the voice of the dwarf at a distance upon the ground, he was satisfied that he had only pulled his own nose to no purpose.

"Good-bye, Manabozho," said the voice of the invisible dwarf. "Count your beaver-tails, and you will find that I have taken another for my sister"; for He of the Little Shell never, in his wanderings or pastimes, forgot his sister and her wishes. "Good-bye, beaver-man!"

And as he went away he made himself visible once

more, and a light beamed about his head and lit the air
around him with a strange splendor; a circumstance
which Manabozho, who was at times quite thick-headed
and dull of apprehension, could in no way understand.

When Dais-Imid returned home, he told his sister
that the time drew nigh when they must separate.

"I must go away," said Dais-Imid, "it is my fate.
You, too," he added, "must go away soon. Tell me
where you would wish to dwell."

She said, "I would like to go to the place of the
breaking of daylight. I have always loved the East.
The earliest glimpses of light are from that quarter,
and it is to my mind the most beautiful part of the
heavens. After I get there, my brother, whenever you
see the clouds, in that direction, of various colors, you
may think that your sister is painting her face."

"And I," said he, "I, my sister, shall live on the
mountains and rocks. There I can see you at the
earliest hour; there the streams of water run clear;
the air is pure; and the golden lights will shine ever
around my head. I shall ever be called 'Puck-Ininee,
or the Little Wild Man of the Mountains.' But," he
resumed, "before we part forever, I must go and try
to find what manitoes rule the earth, and see which of
them will be friendly to us."

He left his sister and traveled over the surface of
the globe, and then went far down into the earth.

He had been treated well wherever he went. But
at last he came to a giant manito, who had a large ket-

tle which was forever boiling. The giant, who was a first cousin to Manabozho, and had already heard of the tricks which Dais-Imid had played upon his kinsman, regarded him with a stern look, and, catching him up in his hand, threw him unceremoniously into the kettle.

It was evidently the giant's intention to drown Dais-Imid. In this he was unsuccessful, for by means of his magic shell, little Dais, in less than a second's time, bailed the water to the bottom, leaped from the kettle, and ran away unharmed.

He returned to his sister and related his rovings and adventures. He finished his story by addressing her thus:

"My sister, there is a manito at each of the four corners of the earth. There is also one above them, far in the sky, a Great Being who assigns to you and to me and to all of us, where we must go. And last," he continued, "there is another and wicked one who lives deep down in the earth. It will be our lot to escape out of his reach. We must now separate. When the winds blow from the four corners of the earth, you must then go. They will carry you to the place you wish. I go to the rocks and mountains, where my kindred will ever delight to dwell."

Dais-Imid then took his ball-stick and commenced running up a high mountain; a bright light shone about his head all the way, and he kept singing as he went:

Blow, winds, blow! my sister lingers
　For her dwelling in the sky,
Where the morn, with rosy fingers,
　Shall her cheeks with vermil dye.

There my earliest views directed,
　Shall from her their color take,
And her smiles, through clouds reflected,
　Guide me on by wood or lake.

While I range the highest mountains,
　Sport in valleys green and low,
Or, beside our Indian fountains,
　Raise my tiny hip-hallo.

His voice rose faintly and more faint, and at last the maiden was alone.

But presently the winds blew, and, as Dais-Imid had predicted, his sister was borne by them to the eastern sky, where she has ever since lived, and her name is now the Morning Star.

VI

OSSEO, THE SON OF THE EVENING STAR

THERE once lived an Indian in the north who had
ten daughters, all of whom grew up to woman-
hood. They were noted for their beauty, especially
Oweenee, the youngest, who was very independent in
her way of thinking. She was a great admirer of
romantic places and spent much of her time with the
flowers and winds and clouds in the open air. It mat-
tered not to her that the flower was homely, if it was
fragrant—that the winds were rough, if they were
healthful—and that the clouds were dark, if they em-
bosomed the fruitful rain; she knew how, in spite of
appearances, to acknowledge the good qualities concealed from the eye.

Her elder sisters were all sought in marriage, and
one after another went off to dwell in the lodges of
their husbands. But Oweenee paid very little attention to the many handsome young men who came to
her father's lodge for the purpose of seeing her. She
was deaf to all proposals, till at last to the great surprise of her kinsfolk she married an old man called
Osseo, who was scarcely able to walk, and who was too

poor to have things like other people. The only property he owned in the world was the walking-staff which
he carried in his hand. But though thus poor and
homely, Osseo was a devout and good man, faithful in
all his duties, and obedient in all things to the Good
Spirit. Of course they jeered and laughed at Oweenee
on all sides, but she seemed to be quite happy, and said
to them:

"It is my choice and you will see in the end who has
acted the wisest."

They made a special mock of the walking-staff, and
scarcely an hour in the day passed that they had not
some disparaging reference to make to it. Among
themselves they spoke of "Osseo of the walking-staff,"
in derision, as one might speak of "the owner of the
big woods," or "the great timberman."

"True," said Oweenee, "it is but a simple stick; but
as it supports the steps of my husband, it is more precious to me than all the forests of the north."

A time came when the sisters and their husbands
and their parents were all invited to a feast. As the
distance was considerable, they doubted whether Osseo,
so aged and feeble, would be able to undertake the
journey; but in spite of their friendly doubts, he joined
them and set out with a good heart.

As they walked along the path they could not help
pitying their young and handsome sister who had such
an unsuitable mate. She, however, smiled upon Osseo,

and kept with him on the way the same as if he had
been the comeliest bridegroom in all the company.
Osseo often stopped and gazed upward; but the others
could perceive nothing in the direction in which he
looked, unless it was the faint glimmering of the evening star. They heard him muttering to himself as they
went along, and one of the elder sisters caught the
words:

"Pity me, my father!"

"Poor old man," said she, "he is talking to his
father. What a pity it is that he would not fall and
break his neck, that our sister might have a young
husband."

Presently as they came to a great rock where Osseo
had been used to breathe his morning and his evening
prayer, the star emitted a brighter ray, which shone
directly in his face. Osseo, with a sharp cry, fell
trembling to the earth, where the others would have
left him. But his good wife raised him up, whereupon
he sprang forward on the path, and with steps light as
the reindeer's he led the party, no longer decrepit and
infirm, but a beautiful young man. All were delighted,
but when they turned around to look for his wife, behold! she had become changed at the same moment into
an aged and feeble woman, bent almost double, and
walking with the staff which he had cast aside.

Osseo immediately joined her, and with looks of
fondness and the tenderest regard bestowed on her

every endearing attention, and constantly addressed
her by the term of "De-ne-moosh-a," or "my sweet-
heart."

As they walked along, whenever they were not gazing
fondly in each other's faces they bent their looks on
heaven, and a light, as if of far-off stars, was in their
eyes.

On arriving at the lodge of the hunter with whom
they were to feast, they found the banquet ready, and
as soon as their entertainer had finished his harangue
—in which he told them his feasting was in honor of
the Evening or Woman's Star—they began to partake
of the portion dealt out to each one of the guests, according to age and character. The food was very
delicious, and they were all happy but Osseo, who
looked at his wife and then gazed upward, as if he
were still looking into the substance of the sky. Then
sounds were heard, as if from far-off voices in the air,
and they became plainer and plainer, till he could
clearly distinguish some of the words.

"My son, my son," said the voice, "I have seen your
afflictions, and pity your wants. I come to call you
away from a scene that is stained with blood and tears.
The earth is full of sorrows. Wicked spirits, the
enemies of mankind, walk abroad and lie in wait to
ensnare the children of the sky. Every night they are
lifting their voices to the Power of Evil, and every day
they make themselves busy in casting mischief in the
hunter's path. You have long been their victim, but

you shall be their victim no more. The spell you were under is broken. Your evil genius is overcome. I have cast him down by my superior strength, and it is this strength I now exert for your happiness. Ascend, my son; ascend into the skies, and partake of the feast I have prepared for you in the stars, and bring with you those you love.

"The food set before you is enchanted and blessed. Fear not to partake of it. It is endowed with magic power to give immortality to mortals and to change men to spirits. Your bowls and kettles shall no longer be wood and earth. The one shall become silver, and the other pure gold. They shall shine like fire, and glisten like the most beautiful scarlet. Every maiden shall also change her state and looks, and no longer be doomed to laborious tasks. She shall put on the beauty of the star-light and become a shining bird of the air. She shall dance and not work. She shall sing, and not cry.

"My beams," continued the voice, "shine faintly on your lodge, but they have power to transform it into the lightness of the skies and decorate it with the colors of the clouds. Come, Osseo, my son, and dwell no longer on earth. Think strongly on my words and look steadfastly at my beams. My power is now at its height. Doubt not, delay not. It is the voice of the Spirit of the Evening Star that calls you away to happiness and celestial rest."

The words were clear to Osseo, but his companions

thought them some far-off sounds of music, or birds singing in the woods. Very soon the lodge began to shake and tremble, and they felt it rising into the air. It was too late to run out, for they were already as high as the tops of the trees. Osseo looked around him as the lodge passed through the topmost boughs, and behold, their wooden dishes were changed into shells of a scarlet color, the poles of the lodge to glittering rods of silver, and the bark that covered them into the gorgeous wings of insects.

A moment more and his brothers and sisters, and their parents and friends, were transformed into birds of various plumage. Some were jays, some partridges and pigeons, and others gay singing birds, who hopped about displaying their many-colored feathers and singing songs of cheerful note.

But his wife, Oweenee, still kept her earthly garb and showed all the signs of extreme old age. He again cast his eyes in the direction of the clouds and uttered the peculiar cry which had given him the victory at the rock. In a moment the youth and beauty of his wife returned; her dingy garments assumed the shining appearance of green silk, and her staff was changed into a silver feather.

The lodge again shook and trembled, for they were now passing through the uppermost clouds, and they immediately afterward found themselves in the Evening Star, the residence of Osseo's father.

"My son," said the old man, "leave the cage of birds

at the door of the lodge.   Then enter, and I will inform
you why you and your wife have been sent for.''

Osseo obeyed, and then took his seat in the lodge.

''Pity was shown to you,'' resumed the King of the
Star, ''on account of the contempt of your wife's sisters, who laughed at her ill fortune and ridiculed you
while you were under the power of that wicked spirit
whom you overcame at the rock.   That spirit lives in
the next lodge, the small star you see on the left of
mine.   He has always felt envious of my family because we had greater power, and especially that we had
committed to us the care of the female world.   He
failed in many attempts to destroy your brothers and
sisters-in-law, but succeeded at last in transforming
yourself and your wife into decrepit old persons.   You
must be careful and not let the light of his beams fall
on you, while you are here, for therein lies the power
of his enchantment.   A ray of light is the bow and
arrow he uses.''

Osseo and Oweenee lived happy and contented in the
parental lodge, and in the course of time had a son,
who grew up rapidly and in the very likeness of Osseo
himself.   He was very quick and ready in learning
everything that was done in his grandfather's dominions, but he wished also to learn the art of hunting, for
he had heard that this was a favorite pursuit below.
To gratify him, his father made him a bow and arrows
and then let the birds out of the cage that he might
practise shooting.   In this pastime he soon became ex-

pert, and the very first day he brought down a bird; but when he went to pick it up, to his amazement it was a beautiful young woman, with the arrow sticking in her breast. It was one of his younger aunts.

The moment her blood fell upon the surface of that pure and spotless planet, the charm was dissolved. The boy immediately found himself sinking, although he was partly upheld by something like wings until he had passed through the lower clouds. He then suddenly dropped upon a high, breezy island in a large lake. He was pleased, on looking up, to see all his aunts and uncles following him in the form of birds, and he soon discovered the silver lodge descending with his father and mother, its waving tassels fluttering like so many insects' gilded wings. It rested on the loftiest cliffs of the island, and there they fixed their residence. They all resumed their natural shapes, but they were diminished to the size of fairies; and as a mark of homage to the King of the Evening Star, they never failed on every pleasant evening during the summer season to join hands and dance upon the top of the rocks. These rocks were quickly observed by the Indians to be covered, on moonlight evenings, with a larger sort of Ininees, or little men. They called them Mish-in-e-mok-in-ok-ong, or Little Spirits, and the island is named from them to this day.

Their shining lodge can be seen in the summer evenings, when the moon beams strongly on the pinnacles of the rocks; and the fishermen who go near those high cliffs at night have even heard the voices of the happy little dancers.   And Osseo and his wife, as fondly attached to each other as ever, always lead the dance.

VII

THE WONDERFUL EXPLOITS OF GRASSHOPPER

A MAN of small stature found himself standing alone on a prairie. He thought to himself:

"How came I here? Are there no beings on this earth but myself? I must travel and see. I must walk till I find the abodes of men."

So soon as his mind was made up, he set out, he knew not whither, in search of habitations. He was a resolute little fellow, and no difficulties could turn him from his purpose; neither prairies, rivers, woods nor storms had the effect to daunt his courage or turn him back. After traveling a long time he came to a wood, in which he saw decayed stumps of trees looking as if they had been cut in ancient times, but aside from that no other trace of men. Pursuing his journey, he found more recent marks of the same kind; after this he came upon fresh traces of human beings; first their footsteps, and then the wood they had felled, lying in heaps. Pushing on, he emerged toward dusk from the forest and beheld at a distance a large village of high lodges standing on rising ground.

"I am tired of this dog-trot," he said to himself. "I will arrive there on a run."

He started off with all his speed. On coming to the first lodge he jumped over it, without any special exertion, and found himself standing by the door on the other side. Those within saw something pass over the opening in the roof; they thought from the shadow it cast that it must have been some huge bird—and then they heard a thump upon the ground.

"What is that?" they all said and several ran out to see.

They invited him in, and he found himself in company with an old chief and several men who were seated in the lodge. Meat was set before him; after which the old chief asked him whither he was going and what was his name. He answered that he was in search of adventures and that his name was "Grasshopper."

They all opened their eyes upon the stranger with a broad stare.

"Grasshopper!" whispered one to another; and a general titter went round.

They invited him to stay with them, which he was inclined to do; for it was a pleasant village, but so small as constantly to embarrass Grasshopper. He was in perpetual trouble; whenever he shook hands with a stranger, to whom he might be introduced, such was the abundance of his strength that, without meaning it he wrung his arm off at the shoulder. Once or twice, in mere sport, he cuffed the boys by the side of the head, and they flew out of sight as though they had been shot from a bow; nor could they ever be found again, though they were searched for in all the country round, far and wide. If Grasshopper proposed to himself a short stroll in the morning, he was at once miles out of town. When he entered a lodge, if he happened for a moment to forget himself, he walked straight through the leathern, or wooden, or earthen walls, as if he had been merely passing through a bush. At his meals he broke in pieces all the dishes, set them down as lightly as he would; and stretching a bit when he rose, it was a common thing for him to push off the top of the lodge.

He wanted more elbow-room; and after a short stay, in which by accidentally letting go of his strength he had nearly laid waste the whole place, filling it with demolished lodges and broken pottery and one-armed men, he made up his mind to go farther, taking with him a young man who had formed a strong attachment for him, and who might serve him as his pipe-bearer. For Grasshopper was a huge smoker, and vast clouds followed him wherever he went; so that people could say, "Grasshopper is coming!" by the mighty smoke he raised.

They set out together, and when his companion was fatigued with walking, Grasshopper would put him forward on his journey a mile or two by giving him a cast in the air and lighting him in a soft place among the trees, or in a cool spot in a water-pond, among the sedges and water-lilies. At other times he would lighten the way by showing off a few tricks, such as leaping over trees, or turning round on one leg till he made the dust fly; at which the pipe-bearer was mightily pleased, although it sometimes happened that the character of these gambols frightened him. For Grasshopper would, without the least hint of such an intention, jump into the air far ahead, and it would cost the little pipe-bearer half a day's hard travel to come up with him. And then, too, the dust Grasshopper raised was often so thick and heavy as completely to bury the poor little pipe-bearer, and compel Grasshopper to dig diligently and with might and main to get him out alive.

One day they came to a very large village, where they were well received. After staying in it some time (in the course of which Grasshopper, in a fit of abstraction, walked straight through the sides of three lodges without stopping to look for the door), they were informed of a number of wicked manitoes or spirits who lived at a distance, and who made it a practise to kill all who came to their lodge. Attempts had been made to destroy them, but they had always proved more than a match for such as had come out against them.

Grasshopper determined to pay them a visit, although he was strongly advised not to do so. The chief of the village warned him of the great danger he would incur, but finding Grasshopper resolved, he said:

"Well, if you will go, being my guest, I will send twenty warriors to serve you."

Grasshopper thanked him for the offer, although he suggested that he thought he could get along without them; at which the little pipe-bearer grinned, for his master had never shown in that village what he could do, and the chief thought that Grasshopper, being little himself, would be likely to need twenty warriors, at the least, to encounter the wicked spirits with any chance of success. So twenty young men made their appearance. They set forward, and after about a day's journey they descried the lodge of the Manitoes.

Grasshopper placed the warriors and his friend, the pipe-bearer, near enough to see all that passed, while he went alone to the lodge.

As he entered, Grasshopper saw five horrid-looking Manitoes in the act of eating. It was the father and his four sons. They were really hideous to look upon. Their eyes were swimming low in their heads, and they glared about as if they were half starved. They offered Grasshopper something to eat, which he politely refused, for he had a strong suspicion that it was the thigh-bone of a man.

"What have you come for?" said the old one.

"Nothing," answered Grasshopper. "Where is your uncle?"

They all stared at him and answered:

"We ate him, yesterday. What do you want?"

"Nothing," said Grasshopper. "Where is your grandfather?"

They all answered, with another broad stare:

"We ate him a week ago. Do you not wish to wrestle?"

"Yes," replied Grasshopper, "I don't mind if I do take a turn; but you must be easy with me, for you see I am very little."

Pipe-bearer, who stood near enough to overhear the conversation, grinned from ear to ear when he caught this remark. The Manitoes answered:

"Oh, yes, we will be easy with you."

And as they said this they looked at one another, and rolled their eyes about in a dreadful manner. A hideous smile came over their faces as they whispered among themselves:

"It's a pity he's so thin." Then, "You go," they said to the eldest brother.

The two got ready—the Manito and Grasshopper—and they were soon clinched in each other's arms for a deadly throw. Grasshopper knew their object—his death; they wanted a taste of his delicate little body, and he was determined they should have it, but perhaps in a different sense from what they intended.

"Haw! haw!" they cried, and soon the dust and dry leaves flew about as if driven by a strong wind. The Manito was strong, but Grasshopper thought he could master him; and all at once giving him a sly trip, just as the wicked spirit was trying to finish his breakfast with a piece out of his shoulder, he sent the Manito head-foremost against a stone; and calling aloud to the three others, he bade them come and take the body away.

The brothers now stepped forth in quick succession, but Grasshopper, having got his blood up and limbered himself by exercise, soon dispatched the three—sending one this way, another that, and the third straight up into the air, so high that he never came down again.

It was time for the old Manito to be frightened, and dreadfully frightened he got, and ran for his life, which was the very worst thing he could have done; for Grasshopper, of all his gifts of strength, was most noted for his speed of foot. The old Manito set off, and for mere sport's sake, Grasshopper pursued him. Sometimes he was before the wicked old spirit, sometimes he was flying over his head, and then he would keep along at a steady trot just at his heels, till he had blown all the breath out of the old knave's body.

Meantime his friend, the pipe-bearer, and the twenty young warriors cried out:

"Ha, ha, ha! ha, ha, ha! Grasshopper is driving the Manito before him."

The Manito only turned his head now and then to look back. At length when he was tired of the sport, Grasshopper, to be rid of him, with a gentle application of his foot sent the wicked old Manito whirling away through the air, where he made a great number of the most curious turn-overs in the world till he came to alight. It so happened, then, that he fell astride of an old bull-buffalo grazing in a distant pasture, who straightway set off with him at a long gallop; and the old Manito has not been heard of to this day.

Then the warriors and the pipe-bearer and Grasshopper set to work and burned down the lodge of the wicked spirits, and when they came to look about, they saw that the ground was strewn on all sides with human bones bleaching in the sun; these were the unhappy victims of the Manitoes. Grasshopper then took three arrows from his girdle, and after having performed a ceremony to the Great Spirit, he shot one into the air, crying:

"You are lying down; rise up, or you will be hit!"

The bones all moved to one place. He shot the second arrow, repeating the same words, and each bone drew toward its fellow-bone. The third arrow brought forth to life the whole multitude of people who had been killed by the Manitoes. Grasshopper conducted the crowd to his friend, the chief of the village, and gave them into his hands, telling who they were and the manner in which they had come to life again. Meanwhile the twenty warriors, pipe-bearer, and all the people cried together:

"Ha, ha, ha! ha, ha, ha! Grasshopper has killed the wicked Manito."

The chief was there with his counsellors, to whom he spoke apart.

"Who is more worthy to rule than you?" said the chief to Grasshopper. "*You* alone can defend us all."

Grasshopper thanked him and told him that he was in search of more adventures.

"I have done some things," said little Grasshopper, rather boastfully, "and I think I can do some more."

The chief still urged him, but he was eager to go, and naming Pipe-bearer to tarry and take his place, Grasshopper set out again on his travels, promising that he would some time or other come back and see them.

"Ho! ho! ho!" they all cried. "Come back again and see us!" He renewed his promise that he would; and then set out alone.

After traveling some time he came to a great lake, and on looking about he discovered a very large otter on an island. He thought to himself, "His skin will make me a fine pouch." And he immediately drew up at long shot and drove an arrow into the otter's side. Then he waded into the lake, and with some difficulty dragged him ashore and up a hill overlooking the lake.

As soon as Grasshopper got the otter into the warm sunshine, he skinned him and threw the carcass some distance off, thinking the war-eagle would come, and that he would have a chance to secure his feathers as ornaments for the head; for Grasshopper began to be proud, and was disposed to display himself.

He soon heard a rushing noise as of a loud wind, but could see nothing. Presently a large eagle dropped, as if from the air, upon the otter's carcass. Grasshopper drew his bow, and the arrow passed through under both of his wings. The bird made a convulsive

flight upward, with such force that the cumbrous body
was borne up several feet from the ground; but the
heavy otter, in which the bird's claws were deeply fixed,
brought the eagle back to the earth. Grasshopper
possessed himself of a handful of the prime feathers,
crowned his head with the trophy, and set off in high
spirits on the look-out for something new.

After walking a while, he came to a body of water
which flooded the trees on its banks—it was a lake
made by beavers. Taking his station on the raised
dam where the stream escaped, he watched to see
whether any of the beavers would show themselves. A
head presently peeped out of the water to see who it
was that disturbed them.

"My friend," said Grasshopper in his most per-
suasive manner, "could you not oblige me by turning
me into a beaver like yourself? Nothing would please
me so much as to make your acquaintance, I can assure you." For Grasshopper was curious to know
how these watery creatures lived. and what kind of
notions they had.

"I do not know," replied the beaver, who was rather
short-nosed and surly. "I will go and ask the others.
Meanwhile stay where you are, if you please."

"To be sure," answered Grasshopper, stealing down
the bank several paces as soon as the beaver's back
was turned.

Presently there was a great splashing of the water,
and all the beavers showed their heads, and looked

warily to where he stood, to see if he was armed. But he had knowingly left his bow and arrows in a hollow tree at a short distance.

After a long conversation, which they conducted in a whisper so that Grasshopper could not catch a word, strain his ears as he would, they all advanced in a body toward the spot where he stood; the chief approaching the nearest and lifting his head highest out of the water.

"Can you not," said Grasshopper, noticing that they waited for him to speak first, "turn me into a beaver? I wish to live among you."

"Yes," answered their chief. "Lie down." And Grasshopper in a moment found himself a beaver, and was gliding into the water, when a thought seemed to strike him, and he paused at the edge of the lake.

"I am very small," he said to the beaver in a sorrowful tone. "You must make me large." For Grasshopper was terribly ambitious and wanted always to be the first person in every company. "Larger than any of you; in my present size it's hardly worth my while to go into the water."

"Yes, yes!" said they. "By and by, when we get into the lodge it shall be done."

They all dived into the lake, and when in passing great heaps of limbs and logs at the bottom, Grasshopper asked their use, they answered, "For our winter's provision."

When they all got into the lodge the number was about one hundred. The lodge was large and warm.

"Now we will make you large," said they. Then, "Will *that* do?"

"Yes," he answered; for he found that he was ten times the size of the largest.

"You need not go out," said the others. "We will bring you food into the lodge, and you will be our chief."

"Very well," Grasshopper answered. He thought, "I will stay here and grow fat at their expense."

But, soon after, one of them ran into the lodge out of breath, crying out:

"We are visited by the Indians!"

All huddled together in great fear. The water began to lower, for the hunters had broken down the dam, and soon they could be heard on the roof of the lodge, breaking it up. Out jumped all the beavers into the water, and so escaped.

Grasshopper tried to follow, then to call them back; but either they did not hear or would not attend to him. So he had to find his own way of getting out. Now, unfortunately, in order to gratify his ambition, the beavers had made him too large to crawl out of the hole. He wiggled and twisted in vain, and only worried himself till the sweat stood out on his forehead in knobs and huge bubbles. He looked like a great bladder swollen and blistered in the sun.

Although he heard and understood every word that the hunters spoke—and some of their expressions suggested terrible ideas—he could not turn himself back into a man. He had chosen to be a beaver, and a beaver he must be. One of the hunters, a prying little man with a single lock dangling over one eye, put his head in at the top of the lodge.

"Ty-au!" cried he. "Tut ty-au! Me-shau-mik—king of beavers is in." Whereupon the whole crowd of hunters began upon him with their clubs, and knocked his skull about until it was no harder than a morass in the middle of summer. Grasshopper thought as well as ever he did, although he was inhabiting the carcass of a beaver; and he felt that he was in a rather foolish scrape.

Presently seven or eight of the hunters hoisted his body upon long poles and marched away home with him. As they went, he reflected in this manner:

"What will become of me? My ghost or shadow will not die after they get me to their lodges. So perhaps then I will be free again."

Invitations were immediately sent out for a grand feast. But as soon as Grasshopper's body got cold, his soul flew off, being uncomfortable in a house without heat.

Having reassumed his mortal shape, Grasshopper found himself standing near a prairie. After walking a distance, he saw a herd of elk feeding. He admired their apparent ease and enjoyment of life, and thought there could be nothing more pleasant than the liberty of running about and feeding on the prairies. He had been a water animal and now he wished to become a land animal, to learn what passed in an elk's head as he roved about. So he asked them if they could not turn him into one of themselves.

"Yes," they answered, after a pause. "Get down on your hands and feet."

He obeyed their directions and forthwith found himself an elk.

"I want big horns, big feet," said he. "I wish to be very large." For all the conceit and vain-glory had not been knocked out of Grasshopper, even by the sturdy thwacks of the hunters' clubs.

"Yes, yes," they answered. "There," exerting their power, "are you big enough?"

"That will do," he replied, for, looking into a lake hard by, Grasshopper saw that he was very large.

The elk spent their time in grazing and running to and fro; but what astonished Grasshopper was that although he often lifted up his head and directed his eyes that way, he could never see the stars, which he had so admired as a human being.

Being rather cold one day, Grasshopper went into a thick wood for shelter, whither he was followed by most of the herd. They had not been long there when some elks from behind passed the others like a strong wind, calling out:

"The hunters are after us!"

All took the alarm, and off they ran, Grasshopper with the rest.

"Keep out on the plains," they said. But it was too late to profit by this advice, for they had already got entangled in the thick woods. Grasshopper soon scented the hunters, who were closely following his trail, for they had left all the other elk and were making after him in full cry. He jumped furiously, dashed through the underwood, and broke down whole groves of saplings in his flight. But this only made it the harder for him to get on, such a huge and lusty elk was he by his own request.

Presently, as he dashed past an open space, he felt an arrow in his side. They could not well miss him, he presented so wide a mark to the shot. He bounded over trees under the smart, but the shafts clattered thicker and thicker at his ribs, and at last one entered his heart. He fell to the ground, and heard the whoop of triumph sounded by the hunters. On coming up, they looked on the carcass with astonishment, and with their hands up to their mouths, exclaimed:

"Ty-au! ty-au!"

There were about sixty in the party, which had come out on a special hunt, as one of their number the day before had observed his large tracks on the plains. Now they were highly elated at having caught this giant elk and immediately set about dividing the spoils. But as soon as the skin was removed, the flesh grew cold. His spirit took its flight from the dead body, and Grasshopper found himself again in human shape, with a bow and arrows.

But his passion for adventure was not yet cooled; for on coming to a large lake with a sandy beach, he saw a large flock of brant. Speaking to them in the brant language, he requested them to make a brant of him.

"Yes," they replied at once, for the brant is a bird of a very obliging disposition.

"But I want to be very large," he said. There was no end to the ambition of little Grasshopper.

"Very well," they answered, and he soon found himself a large brant, all the others standing gazing in astonishment at his great size.

"You must fly as leader," they said.

"No," answered Grasshopper, "I will fly behind."

"Very well," rejoined the brant. "One thing more we have to say to you, brother Grasshopper. You must be careful, in flying, not to look down, or something may happen to you."

"Well, it is so," said he; and soon the flock rose up into the air, for they were bound north. They flew very fast—he behind.

One day, while going with a strong wind and as swiftly as their wings could flap, they passed over a large village. The Indians raised a great shout on seeing them, particularly on Grasshopper's account, for his wings were broader than two large mats. The village people made such a frightful noise that he forgot

what had been told him about looking down. They
were now scudding along as swift as arrows; and as
soon as he brought his neck in and stretched it down to
look at the shouters, his huge tail was caught by the
wind, and over and over he was blown. He tried to
right himself, but without success, for he had no sooner
got out of one heavy air-current than he fell into another, which treated him even more rudely than that
which he had escaped from. Down, down he went,
making more turns than he wished for, from a height
of several miles.

The first moment he had to look about him, Grasshopper, in the shape of a big brant, was aware that he
was jammed into a large hollow tree. To get backward
or forward was out of the question, and there, in spite
of himself, was Grasshopper forced to tarry till his
brant life was ended by starvation, when, his spirit
being at liberty, he was once more a human being.

As he journeyed on in search of further adventures,
Grasshopper came to a lodge in which were two old
men, with heads white from extreme age. They were
very fine old men to look at. There was such sweet-
ness and innocence in their features that Grasshopper
was very glad to accept their invitation to enter the
lodge and tarry a while.

They treated him well, and when he made known to
them that he was going back to his village, his friends
and people, the two white-headed old men very heartily
wished him a good journey and abundance of comfort

in seeing his friends once more. They even arose, old
and infirm as they were, and tottering with exceeding
difficulty to the door, were at great pains to point out
to him the exact course he should take; and called his
attention to the circumstance that it was much shorter
and more direct than the one he would have taken himself. Ah! what merry deceivers were these two old
men with very white heads.

Grasshopper, with blessings showered on him until
he was fairly out of sight, set forth with good heart.
He thought he heard loud laughter resounding after
him in the direction of the lodge; but it could not have
been the two old men, for they were, certainly, too old
to laugh.

He walked briskly all day, and at night he had the
satisfaction of reaching a lodge in all respects like that
which he had left in the morning. There were two
more fine old men, and his treatment was in every particular the same, even down to the parting blessing and
the laughter that followed him as he went his way.

After walking the third day and coming to a lodge
the same as before, he was satisfied from the bearings
of the course he had taken and by a notch which he had
cut in the door-post, that he had been journeying in a
circle, that these were the same two old men, all along,
and that, despite their innocent faces and their very
white heads, they had been playing him a sorry trick.

"Who are you," said Grasshopper, "to treat me so?
Come forth, I say."

They were compelled to obey his summons, lest, in his anger, he should take their lives; and they appeared on the outside of the lodge.

"We must have a little trial of speed, now," said Grasshopper.

"A race?" they asked. "We are very old; we cannot run."

"We will see," said Grasshopper. Whereupon he set them out upon the road and gave them a gentle push, which put them in motion. Then he pushed them again—harder—harder—until they got under fine headway, when he gave each of them an astounding shock with his foot, and off they flew at a great rate, round and round the course; and such was the magic virtue of the foot of Grasshopper, that no object once set a-going by it could by any possibility stop; so that, for aught we know to the contrary, the two innocent, white-headed, merry old men are trotting to this day, with all their might and main around the circle in which they beguiled Grasshopper.

Continuing his journey, Grasshopper, although his head was warm and buzzing with all sorts of schemes, did not know exactly what to do until he came to a big lake. He mounted a high hill to try and see to the other side, but he could not. He then made a canoe and sailed forth. The water was very clear—a transparent blue—and he saw that it abounded with fish of a rare and delicate complexion. This circumstance inspired him with a wish to return to his own village, so that he might bring his people to live near this beautiful lake.

Toward evening, coming to a woody island, he encamped and ate the fish he had speared, and they proved to be as comforting to the stomach as they were pleasing to the eye. The next day Grasshopper returned to the mainland, and as he wandered along the shore he espied at a distance the celebrated giant, Manabozho, who is a bitter enemy of Grasshopper and loses no opportunity to stop him on his journeyings and to thwart his plans.

At first it occurred to Grasshopper to have a trial of wits with the giant, but on second thoughts he said to himself, "I am in a hurry now; I will see him another time."

With no further mischief than raising a great whirlwind of dust, which caused Manabozho to rub his eyes severely, Grasshopper quietly slipped out of the way; and he made good speed withal, for in much less time than you could count half the stars in the sky of a winter night, he had reached home.

His return was welcomed with a great hubbub of feasting and songs; and he had scarcely set foot in the village before he had invitations to take pot-luck at different lodges, and ate enough to have lasted him the rest of his natural life. Pipe-bearer, who had some time before given up the cares of a ruler and fallen back upon his native place, fairly danced with joy at the sight of Grasshopper, who, not to be outdone, dan-

dled him affectionately in his arms by casting him up
and down in the air half a mile or so, till little Pipe-
bearer had no breath left in his body to say that he
was happy to see Grasshopper home again.

Grasshopper gave the village folks a lively account
of his adventures, and when he came to the blue lake
and the abundant fish, he dwelt upon their charms with
such effect that they agreed, with one voice, that it must
be a glorious place to live in, and if he would show them
the way they would shift camp and settle there at once.

He not only showed them the way, but bringing his
wonderful strength and speed of foot to bear, in less
than half a day he had transported the whole village,
with its children, women, tents, and implements of war,
to the new water-side.

Here, for a time, Grasshopper appeared to be content, until one day a message was brought him by a
bear, who said that their king wished to see him immediately at his village. Grasshopper was ready in an
instant; and mounting upon the messenger's back, off
he went. Toward evening they climbed a high mountain and came to a cave where the bear-king lived. He
was a very large person; and puffing with fat and a
sense of his own importance, he made Grasshopper welcome by inviting him into his lodge.

As soon as it was proper, the king spoke, and said
that he had sent for him on hearing that he was the
chief who was moving a large party into the bears'
hunting-ground.

"You must know," said the bear-king with a terrible growl, "that you have no right there, and I wish you would leave the country with your party, or else the strongest force will take possession. This I say."

"Very well," replied Grasshopper, going toward the door, for he suspected that the king of the bears was preparing to give him a hug. "So be it."

He wished to gain time and to consult his people; for he had seen as he came along that the bears were gathering in great force on the side of the mountain. He also made known to the bear-king that he would go back that night so that his people might be put in immediate possession of the royal behest.

The bear-king replied that Grasshopper might do as he pleased, but that one of his young men was at his command; so jumping nimbly on his back, Grasshopper rode home.

He assembled the people and ordered the bear's head off, to be hung outside of the village, that the bear spies, who were lurking in the neighborhood, might see it and carry the news to their chief.

The next morning, by break of day, Grasshopper had all of his young warriors under arms and ready for a fight. And none too soon, for about the middle of the afternoon the bear war-party came in sight, led on by the fat king. The bears advanced on their hind-legs, making a tremendous noise, and a very imposing display of their teeth and eyeballs.

The bear-chief himself came forward, and with a

majestic wave of his right hand, said that he did not
wish to shed the blood of the young warriors; but that
if Grasshopper consented, they two would have a race.
The winner should kill the losing chief, and all his
young men should be servants to the other.

Grasshopper agreed, of course—how little Pipe-
bearer, who stood by, grinned as they came to terms!—
and they started to run before the whole company of
warriors who stood in a circle looking on.

At first there was a prospect that Grasshopper would
be badly beaten; for although he kept crowding the
great fat bear-king till the sweat trickled from his
shaggy ears, he never seemed to be able to push past
him. But by and by, Grasshopper, going through a
number of the most extraordinary maneuvers in the
world, raised about the great fat bear-king such eddies
and whirlwinds of sand, and so danced about, before
and after him, that the king at last got fairly bewildered, and cried out for mercy. But Grasshopper still
went on and reached the goal where he only waited for
the bear-king to come up to drive an arrow through
him. And now in fulfilment of the agreement the bears
must become servants, and Grasshopper ordered them
to take the body off and prepare it for supper.

"I am hungry," he said, "and would hold a great
feast to celebrate our victory."

All the bears had to help, and although bound to act
becomingly according to the forfeit, they made many a
wry face as they carved up the body of their late royal

master. And either by accident or design they fell into many curious blunders. One sprightly young fellow of an inquisitive turn of mind was found upon the roof of the lodge, with his head half-way down the smoke-hole, with a view to learn what they were to have for dinner. Another, a middle-aged bear with very long arms, who was put in charge of the children as nurse while the mothers were outside to look after the preparations, squeezed three or four of the most promising young papooses to death; another, when he should have been waiting at the back of his master, had climbed a shady tree and was indulging in his afternoon nap. And when, at last, the dinner was ready to be served, they came tumbling in with the dishes, heels over head, one after the other, so that one-half of the feast was spread upon the ground, and the other half deposited out of doors, on the other side of the lodge.

After a while, however, by strict discipline and threatening to cut off their provisions, the bear-servants were brought into tolerable control.

Yet Grasshopper, with his ever restless disposition, was uneasy; and, having done so many wonderful things, he resolved upon a strict and thorough reform in all the affairs of the village. To prevent future difficulty, he determined to adopt new regulations between the bears and their masters.

With this view, he issued an edict that henceforward the bears should eat at the first table, and that the Indians were to wait upon them; that in all public processions of an honorable character the bears should go first; and that when any fighting was to be done, the Indians should have the privilege reserved of receiving the first shots. A special exemption was made in behalf of Grasshopper's favorite and confidential adviser, the Pipe-bearer, who had been very busy in private, recommending the new order of things. He was to be allowed to sit at the head of the feast, and to stay at home with the old women in the event of battle.

Having seen his orders strictly enforced and the rights of the bears over the Indians fairly established, Grasshopper fixed his mind upon further adventures. He determined to go abroad for a time, and having an old score to settle with Manabozho, he set out with a hope of soon falling in with that famous giant. Grasshopper was a blood relation of Dais-Imid, or He of the Little Shell, and had heard of what had passed between that giant and his kinsman.

After wandering a long time he came to the lodge of Manabozho, who was absent. He thought he must play him a trick; and so he turned everything in the lodge upside down and killed his birds, of which there was an extraordinary attendance. For Manabozho is master of the fowls of the air, and this was the appointed morning for them to call and pay their court to him. Among the number was a raven, accounted the meanest of birds, which Grasshopper killed and hung up by the neck, as an insult.

He then went on till he came to a very high point of

rocks running out into the lake, from the top of which he could see the country, back as far as the eye could reach. While sitting there, Manabozho's mountain chickens flew around and past him in great numbers. Out of mere spite to their master, Grasshopper shot them by the score, for his arrows were sure and the birds very plenty, and he amused himself by throwing the birds down the rocks. At length a wary bird cried out:

"Grasshopper is killing us; go and tell our father."

Away sped a delegation of the birds which were the quickest of wing, and Manabozho soon made his appearance on the plain below. Grasshopper, who, when he is in the wrong, is no match for Manabozho, made his escape on the other side. Manabozho, who had in two or three strides reached the top of the mountain, cried out:

"You are a rogue. The earth is not so large but I can get up to you."

Off ran Grasshopper and Manabozho after him. The race was sharp; and such leaps and strides as they made! Over hills and prairies with all his speed went Grasshopper, and Manabozho hard upon him. Grasshopper had some mischievous notions still left in his head which he thought might befriend him. He knew that Manabozho was under a spell to restore whatever he, Grasshopper, destroyed. Forthwith he stopped and climbed a large pine-tree, stripped off its beautiful green foliage, threw it to the winds, and then went on.

When Manabozho reached the spot, the tree addressed him:

"Great chief," said the tree, "will you give me my life again? Grasshopper has killed me."

"Yes," replied Manabozho, who, as quickly as he could, gathered the scattered leaves and branches, renewed its beauty with his breath, and set off. Although Grasshopper in the same way compelled Manabozho to lose time in repairing the hemlock, the sycamore, cedar, and many other trees, the giant did not falter, but pushing briskly forward, was fast overtaking him, when Grasshopper happened to see an elk. Asked for old acquaintance' sake, to take him on his back, the elk did so, and for some time made good headway, but still Manabozho was in sight.

He was fast gaining upon him, when Grasshopper threw himself off the elk's back. Striking a great sandstone rock near the path, he broke it into pieces, and scattered the grains in a thousand directions. Manabozho was so close upon him at this place that he had almost caught him; but the foundation of the rock cried out:

"Haye! Ne-me-sho, Grasshopper has spoiled me. Will you not restore me to life?"

"Yes," replied Manabozho, and re-established the rock in all its strength.

He then pushed on in pursuit, and had got so near to Grasshopper as to put out his arm to seize him; but Grasshopper dodged him, and, as his last chance, he immediately raised such a dust and commotion by whirlwinds, as made the trees break and the sand and leaves dance in the air. Again and again Manabozho stretched out his arm, but Grasshopper escaped him at every turn and kept up such a tumult of dust that he was able to dash into a hollow tree which had been blown down, and change himself into a snake without Manabozho's seeing him. He crept out at the roots just in time to save his life, for at that moment Manabozho, who had the power of lightning, struck the tree, and it was strewn about in little pieces.

Again Grasshopper was in human shape, and Manabozho was pressing him hard. At a distance he saw a very high bluff of rocks jutting out into a lake, and he ran for the foot of the precipice, which was abrupt and elevated. As he came near, to his surprise and great relief, the Manito of the rock opened his door and told Grasshopper to come in. The door was no sooner closed than Manabozho knocked.

"Open it!" he cried, with a loud voice.

The Manito was afraid of Manabozho; but he said to Grasshopper:

"Since I have taken you as my guest, I would sooner die with you than open the door."

"Open it!" Manabozho again cried, in a louder voice than before.

The Manito kept silent. Manabozho, however, made no attempt to open it by force. He waited a few moments.

"Very well," he said, "I give you till morning to live."

Grasshopper trembled, for he thought his last hour had come; but the Manito bade him to be of good cheer.

When the night came on the clouds were thick and black, and as they were torn open by the lightning, such discharges of thunder as bellowed forth were never before heard. The clouds advanced slowly and wrapped the earth about with their vast shadows as in a huge cloak. All night long the clouds gathered, and the lightning flashed, and the thunder roared, and above all could be heard Manabozho muttering vengeance upon poor little Grasshopper.

"You have led a very foolish kind of life, Grasshopper," said his friend the Manito.

"I know it—I know it!" Grasshopper answered.

"You had great gifts of strength awarded to you," said the Manito.

"I am aware of it," replied Grasshopper.

"Instead of employing it for useful purposes, and for the good of your fellow-creatures, you have done nothing since you became a man but raise whirlwinds on the highways, leap over trees, break whatever you met in pieces, and perform a thousand idle pranks."

Grasshopper, with great penitence, confessed that his friend the Manito spoke but too truly; and at last his host, with a still more serious manner, said:

"Grasshopper, you still have your gift of strength. Dedicate it to the good of mankind. Lay all of these

wanton and vainglorious notions out of your head.   In
a word, be as good as you are strong.''

"I will," answered Grasshopper.   "My heart is
changed; I see the error of my ways.''

Black and stormy as it had been all night, when
morning came the sun was shining, the air was soft
and sweet as the summer down and the blown rose;
and afar off upon the side of a mountain sat Manabozho, his head upon his knees, languid and cast down
in spirit.   His power was gone, for now Grasshopper
was in the right, and he could touch him no more.

With many thanks Grasshopper left the good Manito,
taking the nearest way home to his own people.

As he passed on, he fell in with an old man who was
wandering about the country in search of some place
which he could not find.   As soon as he learned his difficulty, Grasshopper, placing the old man upon his back,
hurried away, and in a short hour's despatch of foot
set him down among his own kindred, of whom he had
been in quest.

Losing no time, Grasshopper next came to an open
plain where a small number of men stood at bay and on
the very point of being attacked by many armed warriors, fierce of aspect and of prodigious strength.
When Grasshopper saw this unequal struggle, he
rushed forward, seized a long bare pole, and, wielding
it with his whole force, drove the fierce warriors back.
Laying about him on every hand, he soon sent them a
thousand ways in great haste, and in a very sore plight.

Without tarrying to receive the thanks of those to whom he had brought this timely relief, he made his utmost speed, and by the close of the afternoon he had come in sight of his own village. What were his surprise and horror, as he approached nearer, to discover the bears in excellent condition and flesh, seated at lazy leisure in the trees, looking idly on while his brother Indians were dancing a fantastic and wearisome dance, for their pastime, in the course of which they were frequently compelled to go upon all fours and bow their heads in profound obeisance to their bear-masters in the trees.

As he drew nearer, his heart sank within him to see how starved and hollow-eyed and woe-begone they were; and his horror was at its height when, as he entered his own lodge, he beheld his favorite and friend, Pipe-bearer, also on all fours, smoothing the floor with the palms of his hands to make it a comfortable sitting-place for the bears on their return from the dance.

It did not take Grasshopper a long time to resolve what he should do. He immediately resumed power in the village, bestowed a sound cudgeling upon the bears, and sent them off to live in the mountains among their own people, as bears should; restored to his people all their rights; gave them plenty to eat and drink; exerting his great strength in hunting, in rebuilding their lodges, keeping in check their enemies, and doing all the good he could to everybody.

Peace and plenty soon shone and showered upon the

spot; and never once thinking of his wild and wanton frolics, the people blessed Grasshopper for all his kindness, and sincerely prayed that his name might be held in honor for a thousand years to come, as no doubt it will.

Little Pipe-bearer stood by Grasshopper in all his course, and admired his ways as much now that he had taken to being orderly and useful, as in the old times when he was walking a mile a minute, and in mere wantonness bringing home whole forests in his arms for fire-wood, in midsummer.

It was a great old age to which Grasshopper lived, and when at last he came to die, there was not a dry eye in all that part of the world where he spent his latter days.

VIII

THE TOAD-WOMAN

GREAT good luck once happened to a young woman who was living all alone in the woods with nobody near her but her little dog; for she found fresh meat every morning at her door. She was much surprised and very curious to know who it was that supplied her. So she watched one morning, just as the sun had risen, and saw a handsome young man gliding away into the forest. Having seen her, he became her husband, and they had a son.

One evening not long after this, he did not return as usual from hunting. She waited till late at night, but he came not at all.

The next day she swung her child to sleep in its cradle, and then said to her dog, "Take care of your brother while I am gone, and when he cries, halloo for me."

The cradle was made of the finest wampum, and all its bandages and ornaments were of the same precious stuff.

After a short time, the woman heard the cry of the dog, and running home as fast as she could, she found her child gone, and the dog too. On looking around, she saw scattered upon the ground pieces of the wam-prm of her child's cradle, and she knew that the dog had been faithful and had striven his best to save the babe from being carried off.

Now the thief was an old woman from a distant country, called Mukakee Mindemoea, or the Toad-Woman. The mother hurried off at full speed in pursuit of her. As she flew along, she came from time to time to lodges inhabited by old women, who told her at what time the child-thief had passed; they also gave her shoes that she might follow on. A number of these old women seemed to be prophetesses, and knew what was to come long beforehand. Each of them would say to her that when she had arrived at the next lodge, she must set the toes of the moccasins they had given her pointing homeward, and that they would then return of themselves. The young woman was very careful to send back in this manner all the shoes she borrowed.

She thus followed in the pursuit, from valley to valley, and stream to stream, for many months and years, and at length came to the lodge of the last of the friendly old grandmothers, as they were called, who gave her final instructions how to proceed. She told the mother that she was near the place where her son was to be found; and she directed her to build a lodge of cedar-boughs hard by the old Toad-Woman's lodge, and to make a little bark dish, and to fill it with the juice of the wild grape.

"Then," she said, "your first child (meaning the dog) will come and find you out."

These directions the young woman followed just as they had been given to her, and in a short time she heard her son, now grown up, going out to hunt. The dog was following and she called out to him, "Pee-waubik—Spirit-Iron—Twee! Twee!"

The dog came into the lodge, and she set before him the dish of grape-juice.

"See, my child," she said, addressing him, "the pretty drink your mother gives you."

Spirit-Iron took a long draught, and immediately left the lodge with his eyes wide open; for this was the drink which teaches one to see the truth of things as they are. He rose up when he got into the open air, stood upon his hind-legs, and looked about.

"I see how it is," he said; and marching off, erect as a man, he sought out his young master.

Approaching him in great confidence, he bent down and whispered in his ear, having first looked cautiously around to see that no one was listening:

"This old woman here in the lodge is no mother of yours. I have found your real mother, and she is worth looking at. When we come back from our day's sport, I'll prove it to you."

They went out into the woods, and at the close of the afternoon they brought back a great spoil of meat of all kinds. Then the young man, as soon as he had laid aside his weapons, said to the old Toad-Woman, "Send some of the best of this meat to the stranger who has arrived lately."

The Toad-Woman answered, "No! Why should I send to her, the poor widow!" But the young man would not be refused; and at last the old Toad-Woman consented to take something and throw it down at the door.

"My son gives you this," she called out. But, being bewitched by Mukakee Mindemoea, the meat was so bitter and distasteful that the young woman immediately cast it out of the lodge after her.

In the evening the young man paid the stranger a visit at her lodge of cedar-boughs. She then told him that she was his real mother, and that he had been stolen away from her by the old Toad-Woman, who was a child-thief and a witch. As the young man appeared to doubt, she said to him: "Feign yourself sick when you go home to her lodge; and when the Toad-Woman asks what ails you, say that you wish to see your cradle; for your cradle was of wampum, and your faithful brother the dog, in striving to save you, tore off these pieces which I show you."

They were real wampum, white and blue, shining and beautiful; and the young man, placing them in his bosom, set off. He did not seem quite steady in his belief of the strange woman's story. But the dog, Spirit-Iron, taking his arm, kept close by his side and gave him many words of encouragement as they went along. They entered the lodge together; and the old Toad-Woman saw, from something in the dog's eye, that trouble was coming.

"Mother," said the young man, placing his hand to his head and leaning heavily upon Spirit-Iron, as if a sudden faintness had come upon him, "Why am I so different in looks from the rest of your children?"

"Oh," she answered, "there was a very bright, clear blue sky when you were born; that is the reason."

He seemed to be so very ill that the Toad-Woman at length asked what she could do for him. He said that nothing could do him good but the sight of his cradle. She ran immediately and brought a cedar cradle; but he said:

"That is not my cradle."

She went and got another of her own children's cradles, of which there were four; but he turned his head and said:

"That is not mine; I am as sick as ever."

When she had shown the four, and they had all been rejected, she at last produced the real cradle. The young man saw that it was of the same stuff as the wampum which he had in his bosom. He could even see the marks of the teeth of Spirit-Iron left upon the edges, where he had taken hold, striving to hold it back. So he had no doubt, now, which was his mother.

To get free of the old Toad-Woman, it was necessary that the young man should kill a fat bear; and, being directed by Spirit-Iron, who was very wise in such a matter, he secured the fattest in all that country. Having stripped a tall pine of all its bark and branches, he perched the carcass in the top, with its head to the east and its tail due west. Then returning to the lodge, he informed the old Toad-Woman that the fat bear was ready for her, but that to get it she would have to go very far, even to the end of the earth. She answered:

"It is not so far but that I can get it!" For of all things in the world, a fat bear was the delight of the old Toad-Woman.

She at once set forth; and she was no sooner out of sight than the young man and his dog, Spirit-Iron, blew a strong breath in the face of the Toad-Woman's four children (who were all bad spirits, or bear-fiends), and so put out their life. Then setting them up by the side of the door, they thrust a piece of the white bear-fat in each of their mouths.

The Toad-Woman spent a long time in finding the bear which she had been sent after, and she made at least five and twenty attempts before she was able to climb to the carcass. She slipped down three times where she went up once. But at last she succeeded and returned with the great bear on her back. As she drew near her lodge she was astonished to see the four children standing up by the door-posts with the fat in their mouths. She was angry with them, and called out:

"Why do you thus insult the pomatum of your brother?"

She was still more angry when they made no answer to her complaint; but when she found that they were stark dead and had been placed in this way to mock her,

her fury was very great indeed. She ran after the tracks of the young man and his mother as fast as she could; so fast, indeed, that she was on the very point of overtaking them, when the dog, Spirit-Iron, coming close up to his master, whispered to him—"Snake-berry!"

"Let the snakeberry spring up to detain her!" cried out the young man. And immediately the berries spread for a long distance like scarlet all over the path, and the old Toad-Woman, who was almost as fond of these berries as she was of fat bears, could not avoid stooping down to pick and eat.

The old Toad-Woman was very anxious to get forward, but the snakeberry-vines kept spreading out on every side; and they grew and grew, and spread and spread. And to this day the wicked old Toad-Woman is busy picking the berries. She will never be able to get beyond to the other side, to disturb the happiness of the young hunter and his mother, who still live, with their faithful dog, in the shadow of the beautiful wood-side where they were born.

IX

THE ORIGIN OF THE ROBIN

AN old man had an only son, named Iadilla, who had come to that age when it is thought to be time for a boy to make the long and final fast which is to secure through life a guardian genius or spirit. The father was ambitious that his son should surpass all others in whatever was deemed wisest and greatest among his people. He thought it necessary that the young Iadilla, to do this, should fast a much longer time than any of those renowned for their power or wisdom. The father therefore directed his son to prepare with great ceremony for the important event. First he was to go several times to the sweating-lodge and bath, which were to prepare and purify him for communion with his good spirit. Then he was to lie down upon a clean mat in a little lodge expressly provided for him. He was especially enjoined, at the same time, to endure his fast like a man, and promised that at the end of twelve days he should receive food and the blessing of his father.

The lad carefully observed these commands, and lay with his face covered, calmly awaiting the approach of the spirit which was to decide his good or evil fortune for all the days of his life.

Every morning his father came to the door of the little lodge and encouraged him to persevere, dwelling at length on the vast honor and renown that must ever attend him, should he accomplish the full term of trial allotted to him.

To these glowing words of promise and glory the boy never replied, but he lay without the least sign of discontent or murmuring until the ninth day, when he addressed his father as follows:

"My father, my dreams forbode evil. May I break my fast now, and at a more favorable time make a new fast?"

The father answered:

"My son, you know not what you ask. If you get up now, all your glory will depart. Wait patiently a little longer. You have but three days more, and your term will be completed. You know it is for your own good, and I encourage you to persevere. Shall not your aged father live to see you a star among the chieftains and the beloved of battle?"

The son assented; and covering himself more closely, that he might shut out the light which prompted him to complain, he lay till the eleventh day, when he repeated his request.

The father addressed Iadilla as he had the day before, and promised that he would himself prepare his first meal and bring it to him by the dawn of the next morning.

The son moaned, and the father added:

"Will you bring shame upon your father when his sun is falling in the west?"

"I will not shame you, my father," replied Iadilla; and he lay so still and motionless that you could only know that he was living by the gentle heaving of his breast.

At the spring of day, the father, delighted at having gained his end, prepared a repast for his son and hastened to set it before him. But on coming to the door of the little lodge, he was surprised to hear his son talking to himself. He stooped his ear to listen, and, looking through a small opening, was yet more astonished when he beheld his son painted with vermillion over all his breast. He was just in the act of finishing his work by laying on the paint as far back on his shoulders as he could reach, saying at the same time to himself:

"My father has destroyed my fortune as a man. He would not listen to my requests. He has urged me beyond my tender strength. He will be the loser. I shall be forever happy in my new state, for I have been obedient to my parent. He alone will be the sufferer, for my guardian spirit is a just one. Though not propitious to me in the manner I desired, he has shown me pity in another way—he has given me another shape; and now I must go."

At this moment the old man broke in, exclaiming:

"My son! my son! I pray you leave me not!"

But the young man, with the quickness of a bird, had flown to the top of the lodge and perched himself on the highest pole, having been changed into a beautiful robin red-breast. He looked down upon his father with pity beaming in his eyes, and addressed him as follows:

"Regret not, my father, the change you behold. I shall be happier in my present state than I could have been as a man. I shall always be the friend of men and keep near their dwellings. I shall ever be happy and contented; and although I could not be a mighty warrior as you wished, it will be my daily aim to make you amends for it as a harbinger of peace and joy. I will cheer you by my songs and strive to inspire in others the joy and lightsomeness of heart I feel in my present state. This will be some compensation to you for the loss of glory you expected. I am now free from the cares and pains of human life. My food is spontaneously furnished by the mountains and fields, and my path of life is in the bright air."

Then stretching himself on his toes, as if delighted with the gift of wings, Iadilla carolled one of his sweetest songs and flew away into a neighboring wood.

X

WHITE FEATHER AND THE SIX GIANTS

THERE was an old man living in the depth of a forest with his grandson, whom he had taken in charge when quite an infant. The child had no parents, brothers, or sisters; they had all been destroyed by six large giants, and he was informed that he had no other relative living besides his grandfather. The band of Indians to whom he had belonged had put up their children on a wager in a race against those of the giants, and had thus lost them. But there was an old tradition in the tribe, that one day it would produce a great man, who would wear a white feather, and who would astonish every one by his feats of skill and bravery.

The grandfather, as soon as the child could play about, gave him a bow and arrows to amuse himself with. He went into the edge of the woods one day and saw a rabbit; but not knowing what it was, he ran home and described it to his grandfather, who told him that its flesh was good to eat, and that if he would shoot one of his arrows into its body he would kill it. The boy went out again and brought home the little animal, which he asked his grandfather to boil, that they might feast on it. The old man humored the boy in this and encouraged him to go on acquiring the knowledge of hunting, until he could kill deer and the larger kinds of game. And thus he became, as he grew up, an expert hunter.

As they lived alone, and away from other Indians, the curiosity of the stripling was excited to know what was passing in the world. One day he came to the edge of a prairie, where he saw ashes like those at his grandfather's lodge, and lodge-poles left standing. He returned and inquired whether his grandfather had put up the poles and made the fire.

"No," answered the old man, "nor do I believe that you have seen anything of the kind; you must have lost your sense to be thinking of such things."

Another day the youth went out to see what there was, within a day's hunt, that was curious; and on entering the woods he heard a voice calling out to him:

"Come here, you who are destined to wear the White Feather. You do not wear it, yet, but you are worthy of it. Return home and take a short nap. You will dream of hearing a voice, which will tell you to rise and smoke. You will see in your dream a pipe, a smoking-sack, and a large white feather. When you awake you will find these articles. Put the feather on your head, and you will become a great hunter, a great warrior, and a great man, able to do anything. As a proof that these things shall come to pass, when you smoke, the smoke will turn into pigeons."

The voice then informed the youth who he was, and made known the character of his grandfather, who was imposing upon him to serve his own ends.

The voice-spirit then caused a vine to be laid at his side, and told him that he was now of an age to avenge the wrongs of his kindred.

"When you meet your enemy," the spirit added, "you will run a race with him. He will not see the vine, because it is enchanted. While you are running, you will throw it over his head and entangle him, so that you will win the race."

Long before this speech was ended the youth had turned to the quarter from which the voice proceeded, and was astonished to behold a man; as yet he had never seen any human being besides his grandfather.

As he looked more keenly, he saw that this man, who had the looks of great age, was wood from the breast downward, and that he appeared to be fixed in the earth. As the youth's eye dwelt upon this strange being, the countenance by degrees faded away, and when he advanced to the spot whence it had addressed him, it was gone.

He returned home; slept, and in the midst of his slumbers, as from the hollow of the air, heard the voice; wakened and found the promised gifts. It was all just as the old man had said. The grandfather on awakening was greatly surprised to find the youth with a white feather on his forehead, and to see flocks of pigeons flying out of the lodge. He then remembered the old tradition, and knowing that now the day had come when he should lose control of his charge, he bitterly bewailed the hour.

Possessed of his three magic gifts, the young man departed the next morning, to seek his enemies and to demand revenge.

The six giants lived in a very high lodge in the middle of a wood. He traveled on with good heart till he reached this lodge, where he found that his coming had been made known by the little spirits who carry the news. The giants hastened out and gave a cry of joy as they saw him drawing near. When he approached within hail, they began to make sport of him, saying:

"Here comes the little man with the white feather, who is to achieve such wonderful wonders."

When, however, he had arrived among them, they spoke him fair, saying he was a brave man and would do brave things. Their object was to encourage him, so that he would be bold to engage in some foolhardy trial of strength.

Without paying much heed to their fine speeches, White Feather went fearlessly into their lodge; and without waiting for invitation, he challenged them to a foot-match. They agreed; and by way of being easy at first, told him to begin the race with the smallest of their number.

The point to which they were to run was a peeled tree toward the rising sun, and then back to the starting-

place, which was a war-club of iron. Whoever won this
stake was empowered to use it in despatching the de-
feated champion. If White Feather should overcome
the first giant, he was to try the second, and so on, until
they had all measured speed with him. To this the
giants agreed without a thought that he would survive
the first trial. But White Feather feared nothing and,
by a dexterous use of the vine, gained the race, struck
down his competitor, and cut off his head.

The next morning he raced with the second giant,
whom he also outran, killed and beheaded.

He went on in this way for five mornings, always
conquering by the aid of his vine, and lopping off the
heads of the vanquished.

Finally the last of the giants who was yet to run with
him acknowledged his power, but prepared secretly to
deceive him. By way of parley, he proposed that
White Feather should leave the heads with him, and
offered to give him a handsome start for odds. This
White Feather declined, as he preferred to keep the
heads as trophies of his victory.

On his way to the giant's lodge the sixth morning,
White Feather met his old counsellor in the woods.
He was standing rooted in the earth, as before. He
told White Feather that he was about to give him a
word of warning.

"On your way this morning," he said, "you will meet
the most beautiful woman in the world, but do not trust
her or pay the least attention to her. As soon as you

catch her eye you must wish yourself changed into an elk. The change will take place immediately. Do not look at her again.''

White Feather thanked his kind adviser, who even as he spoke was disappearing as before, then proceeded toward the lodge. He had not gone far before he met the maiden, who was, indeed, as lovely as the morning's light. This was White Feather's first sight of a maiden, and he was greatly disposed to linger. But remembering the counsellor's words, he lost no time in becoming an elk. At this the maiden began to reproach him that he had cast aside the form of a man so that he might avoid her.

''I have traveled a great distance,'' she said, ''to see you and to become your wife; for I have heard of your great achievements and admire you very much.''

Now this woman was the sixth giant, who had assumed this disguise to entrap White Feather. But without a suspicion of her real character, her reproaches and her beauty affected him so deeply that he wished himself a man again, and at once resumed his natural shape. Then they sat down and began to talk together.

Soothed by her smiles and gracious manner, he laid his head on her lap, and in a little while fell into a deep slumber.

Even then, such was her fear of White Feather, she doubted whether his sleep might not be feigned. To assure herself she pushed his head aside, and seeing

that he remained unconscious, she quickly assumed the
form of the sixth giant. He took the plume from the
brow of White Feather and placed it upon his own
head. Then with a sudden blow of his war-club the
giant changed White Feather into a dog, in which form
he followed his enemy to the lodge.

While these things were passing, there were living
in an Indian village at some distance two sisters, the
daughters of a chief. These sisters were rivals, and
they were at that very time fasting to acquire power
for enticing the wearer of the white feather to visit
their lodge. They each secretly hoped to win his love,
and each had built a lodge on the border of the village
encampment.

The giant, knowing this and having become possessed of the magic plume, went immediately to visit
them. As he approached, the sisters, who were on the
look-out at their lodge-doors, espied and recognized
the feather.

The elder sister had prepared her lodge with great
show, and all the finery she could command, so as to
attract the eye. The younger touched nothing in her
lodge, but left it in its ordinary state.

The elder went out to meet the giant and invited him
in. He accepted her invitation and made her his wife.
The younger sister invited the enchanted dog into her
lodge, prepared him a good supper and a neat bed, and
treated him with much attention.

The giant, supposing that whoever possessed the

white feather possessed also all its virtues, went out upon the prairie to hunt, hallooing aloud to the game to come and be killed; but the great hubbub he kept up scared them away, and he returned at night with nothing but himself; for he had shouted so lustily all day long that he had been obliged to leave even the mighty halloo behind.

The dog went out the same day hunting upon the banks of a river. He stole quietly along to a certain spot, and stepping into the water drew out a stone, which instantly became a beaver.

The next day the giant followed the dog, and hiding behind a tree, watched the manner in which the dog hunted in the river and drew out a stone, which at once turned into a beaver.

"Ah, ha!" said the giant to himself, "I will catch some beaver for myself."

So as soon as the dog had left the place, the giant went to the river, and, imitating the dog, drew out a stone. He was delighted to see it change into a fine fat beaver as soon as it touched the land.

Tying it to his belt he hastened home, shouting a good deal and brandishing the white feather about, as if he were prepared now to show them what he could do when he once tried. And when he reached home he threw the beaver down, as is the custom, at the door of the lodge before he entered.

After being seated a short time, he gave a dry cough and bade his wife bring in his hunting girdle. She made despatch to obey him and presently returned with the girdle, with nothing tied to it but a stone.

The next day the dog, finding that his method of catching beavers had been discovered, went to a wood at some distance and broke off a charred limb from a burned tree. This limb instantly became a bear. The giant, who appeared to have lost faith in his hullaba-looing, again watched him, did exactly as the dog had done, and carried a bear home; but his wife, when she came to go out for it, found nothing but a black stick tied to his belt.

And so it happened with everything. Whatever the dog undertook, prospered; whatever the giant attempted, failed. And even his brave halloo had now died away to a feeble chirp. Every day the younger sister had reason to be more proud of the poor dog she had asked into her lodge, and every day the elder sister was made more aware that, though she had married the white feather, the virtues of the magic plume were not the personal property of the noisy giant.

At last the wife determined that she would go to her father and make known to him what a valuable husband she had, and how he furnished her lodge with a great abundance of sticks and stones, which he would pass upon her for bear and beaver. So, when her husband had started for the hunt, she set out.

As soon as these two had gone away from the neighborhood, the dog made signs to his mistress to sweat him after the manner of the Indians. He had always

been a good dog, and she was willing to oblige him.
She accordingly made a lodge just large enough for
him to creep in. She then put in heated stones and
poured water upon them, raising a vapor that filled
the lodge and searched with its warmth to the very
heart's core of the enchanted dog.

When this had been kept up for the customary time,
the enchanted dog was completely sweated away, and
out came in his stead a very handsome young man.
But unhappily he was without the power of speech. In
taking away the form of the dog, it appears that the
sweating-lodge had also carried off his voice with it.

Meantime the elder sister had reached her father's
lodge and had told him with much circumstance and a
very long face how her sister was supporting an idle
dog, and entertaining him as her husband. In her
anxiety to make known her sister's affairs and the great
scandal she was bringing upon the family, the elder sister forgot to say anything of the sticks and stones
which her own husband brought home for bears and
beavers. The old man listening to his daughter and
suspecting that there was magic about, sent a deputation of young men and women to ask his younger
daughter to come to him and to bring her dog along
with her. When the deputation reached the lodge,
they were surprised to find in the place of the dog a
fine young man; and on announcing their message,
they all returned to the old chief, who was no less surprised at the change.

He immediately assembled all the old and wise heads
of the nation to come and be witnesses to the exploits
which it was reported that the young man could perform. The sixth giant, although neither very old nor
very wise, thrust himself in among the relations of the
old chief.

When they were all assembled and seated in a circle,
the old chief took his pipe and filled it, and passed it
to the Indians around, to see if anything would happen
when they smoked. They passed it on until it came to
the Dog, who made a sign that it should be handed first
to the giant, and this was done. And the giant puffed
with all his might, and shook the white feather upon
his head, and swelled his chest; but nothing came of it,
except a great deal of smoke. The Dog then took it
himself. He made a sign to them to put the white
feather upon his head. This was no sooner done than
he recovered his speech, and, beginning to draw upon
the pipe at the same moment, behold! immense flocks of
white and blue pigeons rushed from the smoke. Then
White Feather, at the request of the company, faith-
fully recounted his history, and the sixth giant was
known for what he was. So the old chief, who was a
magician too, ordered that he should be transformed
into a dog and turned into the middle of the village,
where the boys could pelt him to death with clubs.
This being done, the whole six giants were at an end,
and never troubled that neighborhood again, forever
after.

The chief then gave out a further command, at the request of White Feather, that all the young men should employ themselves four days in making arrows. White Feather also asked for a buffalo robe. This he cut into thin shreds, and in the night went secretly and sowed them about the prairie in every direction.

At the end of the four days he invited the young men to gather together all of their arrows and to accompany him to a buffalo hunt. When they got out upon the prairie, they found it covered with a great herd of buffalos. Of these they killed as many as they pleased, and afterward they had a grand festival in honor of White Feather's triumph over the giants.

All this being pleasantly over, White Feather got his wife to ask her father's permission to go with him on a visit to his grandfather. The old chief replied that a woman must follow her husband into whatever quarter of the world he may choose to go.

So bidding farewell to all his friends, White Feather placed the plume in his frontlet, took his war-club in his hand, and led the way into the forest, followed by his faithful wife.

XI

THE MAGIC PACKET

A POOR man, called Iena, or the Wanderer, was in
the habit of roaming about from place to place,
forlorn, without relations, and almost helpless. He
had often wished for a companion to share his solitude;
but who would think of joining his fortunes with those
of a poor wanderer, who had no shelter in the world
but such as his leather hunting-shirt provided, and no
other household than the packet in which his hunting-
shirt was laid away?

One day Iena hung up his packet on the branch of
a tree, and then set out in quest of game.

On returning to the spot in the evening, he was surprised to find a small but neat lodge built in the place
where he had left his packet; and on looking in he beheld a beautiful maiden sitting on the further side of
the lodge, with his packet lying beside her.

During the day Iena had so far prospered in his
sport as to kill a deer, which he now cast down at the
lodge-door.

The maiden did not pause to take the least notice of
the hunter, or to give him a word of welcome, but ran
out to see whether it was a large deer that he had

brought. In her haste she stumbled and fell at the threshold.

Iena looked at her with astonishment, and thought to himself, "I supposed I was blessed, but I find my mistake. Night-Hawk," said he, speaking aloud, "I will leave my game with you that you may feast on it."

He then took up his packet and departed. After walking some time he came to another tree, on which he suspended his packet, as before, and the following morning went for the second time in search of game.

Success again attended him, and he returned, bringing with him a deer. He found that a lodge had sprung up as before, just where he had hung his packet. He looked in and saw a beautiful maiden sitting alone, with his packet by her side.

She arose and came out toward the deer which he had deposited at the door, and he immediately went into the lodge and sat by the fire, as he was weary with the day's hunt, which had carried him far away.

The woman did not return, and wondering at her delay, Iena at last arose, peeped through the door of the lodge and beheld her greedily eating all the fat of the deer. He exclaimed:

"I thought I was blessed, but I find I was mistaken." Then addressing the woman, "Poor Marten," said he, "feast on the game I have brought."

He again took up his packet and departed. Then finding a tree, he hung it upon a branch, and the next morning again wandered off in quest of game.

In the evening he returned, with his customary good luck, bringing in a fine deer, and again found that a lodge had taken the place of his packet. He gazed through an opening in the side of the lodge, and there was another beautiful woman sitting alone, with his packet by her side.

"Oh!" he exclaimed, "it is the same as it was yesterday and the day before that. I am Iena, the Wanderer, and it is not the will of the Great Spirit that he should have a lodge, a woman, or the fat of the deer that he kills."

So saying he entered the lodge, but the woman rose cheerfully, welcomed him home, and without delay or complaining brought in the deer, cut it up as it should be, and hung up the meat to dry. She then prepared a portion of it for the supper of the weary hunter, who was thinking to himself, "Now I am certainly blessed."

And so it went on. He continued his practise of hunting every day, and the woman, on his return, always welcomed him, readily took charge of the meat, and promptly prepared his evening meal; and he ever after lived a contented and happy man.

XII

THE MAN WITH HIS LEG TIED UP

A S a punishment for having once upon a time used that foot against a venerable medicine man, Aggo Dah Gauda had one leg looped up to his thigh, so that he was obliged to get along by hopping. By dint of practise he had become very skilful in this exercise, and he could make leaps which seemed almost incredible.

Aggo had a beautiful daughter, and his chief care was to secure her from being carried off by the king of the buffalos, who was the ruler of all the herds of that kind, and had them entirely at his command to make them do as he willed.

Dah Gauda, too, was quite an important person in his own way, for he lived in great state, having a log house of his own and a court-yard which extended from the sill of his front-door as many hundred miles westward as he chose to measure it.

Although he might claim this extensive privilege of ground, he advised his daughter to keep within doors, and by no means to go far in the neighborhood. Otherwise she would be sure to be stolen away, as he was satisfied that the buffalo-king spent night and day lurking about, lying in wait to seize her.

One sunshiny morning, when there were just two or three promising clouds rolling moistly about the sky, Aggo prepared to go out a-fishing; but before he left the lodge he reminded her of her strange and industrious lover, whom she had never seen.

"My daughter," said he, "I am going out to fish, and as the day will be a pleasant one, you must recollect that we have an enemy near, who is constantly going about with two eyes that never close. Do not expose yourself out of the lodge."

With this excellent advice, Aggo hopped off in high spirits. But he had scarcely reached the fishing-ground, when he heard a voice singing at a distance:

> Man with the leg tied up,
> Man with the leg tied up,
> Broken hip—hip—
> Hipped.

> Man with the leg tied up,
> Man with the leg tied up,
> Broken leg—leg—
> Legged.

There was no one in sight, but Aggo heard the words quite plainly, and as he suspected the ditty to be the work of his enemies, the buffalos, he hopped home as fast as his one leg could carry him.

Meantime, the daughter had no sooner been left alone in the lodge than she thought to herself:

"It is hard to be thus forever kept in doors. But my father says it would be dangerous to venture

abroad. I know what I will do. I will get on the top
of the house, and there I can comb and dress my hair,
and no one can harm me.''

She accordingly ascended the roof and busied herself in untying and combing her beautiful hair; for it
was truly beautiful, not only of a fine, glossy quality,
but so very long that it hung over the eaves of the
house and reached down to the ground, as she sat
dressing it.

She was wholly occupied in this employment, without
a thought of danger, when all of a sudden the king of
the buffalos came dashing up with his herd of followers. Making sure of her by means of her drooping
tresses, he placed her upon the back of one of his
favorite buffalos, and away he cantered over the
plains. Plunging into a river that bounded his land,
he bore her safely to his lodge on the other side.

And now the buffalo-king, having secured the beautiful person of Aggo Dah Gauda's daughter, set to
work to make her heart his own—a little ceremony
which it would have been, perhaps, wiser for his majesty, the king of the buffalos, to have attended to before
he carried her off, for he now worked to little purpose.
Although he labored with great zeal to gain her affections, she sat pensive and disconsolate in the lodge
among the other women. She scarcely ever spoke, nor
did she take the least interest in the affairs of the
king's household.

To the king himself she paid no heed, and although

he breathed forth to her every soft and gentle word he could think of, she sat still and motionless, for all the world like one of the lowly bushes by the door of her father's lodge when the summer wind had died away.

The king enjoined it upon the others in the lodge as a special edict, on pain of instant death, to give to Aggo's daughter everything that she wanted, and to be careful not to displease her. They set before her the choicest food. They gave her the seat of honor in the lodge. The king himself went out hunting to obtain the most dainty meats, both of animals and wild fowl, to pleasure her palate; and he treated her every morning to a ride upon one of the royal buffalos, who was so gentle in his motions as not even to disturb a single one the tresses of the beautiful hair of Aggo's daughter as she paced along.

And not content with these proofs of his attachment, the king would sometimes fast from all food, and having thus purified his spirit and cleared his voice, he would take his Indian flute, sit before the lodge, and give vent to his feelings in pensive echoes, something after this fashion:

> My sweetheart,
> My sweetheart,
>   Ah me!
> When I think of you,
> When I think of you,
>   Ah me!
> What can I do, do, do?

How I love you,
How I love you,
  Ah me!
Do not hate me,
Do not hate me,
  Ah me!
Speak—e'en berate me.
When I think of you,
  Ah me!
What can I do, do, do?

In the meantime, Aggo Dah Gauda reached home, and finding that his daughter had been stolen, was so thoroughly aroused that he would have forthwith torn every hair from his head in indignation, had he not been entirely bald. This relief being out of the question, Aggo hopped off half a mile in every direction as an easy and natural vent to his feelings. First he hopped east, then he hopped west, next he hopped north, and again he hopped south, all in search of his daughter; till the one leg was fairly tired out. Then he sat down in his lodge, and resting himself a little, reflected. After that he vowed that his single leg should never know rest again until he had found his beautiful daughter and brought her home. For this purpose he immediately set out.

Now that he proceeded more coolly, he could easily track the buffalo-king until he came to the banks of the river, where he saw that he had plunged in and swum over. There having been a frosty night or two since, the water was so covered with thin ice that Aggo could not venture upon it, even with one leg. So he encamped hard by till it became more solid, and then crossed over and pursued the trail.

As he went along he saw branches broken off and strewed behind, which guided him in his course; for these had been purposely cast along by the daughter. And the manner in which she had accomplished it was this. Her hair was all untied when she was caught up, and being very long it took hold of the branches as they darted along, and it was these twigs that she broke off as signs to her father.

When Aggo came to the king's lodge it was evening. Carefully approaching, he peeped through the sides, and saw his daughter sitting disconsolate. She immediately caught his eye, and knowing that it was her father come for her, she all at once appeared to relent in her heart. Asking for the royal dipper, she said to the king:

"I will go and get you a drink of water."

This token of submission delighted his majesty, and, high in hope, he waited with impatience for her return.

Some time passed and at last he went out; but nothing could be seen or heard of the captive daughter. Then calling together his followers, he sallied forth with them upon the plains. They had not gone far when they espied by the light of the moon, which was shining roundly just over the edge of the prairie, Aggo Dah Gauda, his daughter in his arms, making all speed with his one leg toward the west.

The buffalo, set on by their king, raised a great shout and scampered off in pursuit. They thought to overtake Aggo in less than no time; but although he had a single leg only, it was in such fine condition to go, that to every pace of theirs he hopped the length of a cedar-tree.

But the buffalo-king was well assured that he would be able to overtake Aggo, hop as briskly as he might. It would be a mortal shame, thought the king, to be outstripped by a man with one leg tied up; so, shouting and cheering and issuing orders on all sides, he set the swiftest of his herd upon the track, with strict commands to take Aggo dead or alive. And a curious sight it was to see.

At one time a buffalo would gain handsomely upon Aggo, and be just at the point of laying hold of him, when off Aggo would hop, a good furlong, in an oblique line, wide out of his reach; which bringing him nearly in contact with another of the herd, away he would go again, just as far off in another direction.

And in this way Aggo kept the whole company of the buffalos zigzagging across the plain, with the poor king at their head, running to and fro, shouting among them and hurrying them about in the wildest way. It was an extraordinary road that Aggo was taking toward home; and after a time it so puzzled and be-

wildered the buffalos that they were driven half out
of their wits, and they roared and brandished their
tails and foamed, as if they would put out of countenance and frighten out of sight the old man in the
moon, who was looking on all the time, just above the
edge of the prairie.

As for the king himself, he lost all patience at last
at the absurd idea of chasing a man with one leg all
night long, so calling his herd together, he fled in disgust toward the west, and never more appeared in all
that part of the country.

Aggo, relieved of his pursuers, hopped off a hundred
steps in one, till he reached the stream, crossed it in a
twinkling of the eye, and bore his daughter in triumph
to his lodge. .

In the course of time Aggo's beautiful daughter
married a very worthy young warrior, who was neither
a buffalo-king nor so much as the owner of any more
of the buffalos than a splendid skin robe which he
wore, with great effect, thrown over his shoulders, on
his wedding-day. On which occasion, Aggo Dah
Gauda hopped about on his one leg livelier than ever.

XIII

LEELINAU, THE LOST DAUGHTER

LEELINAU was the favorite daughter of a hunter, who lived on the lake shore near the base of the lofty highlands called Kaug Wudjoo.

From her earliest youth Leelinau was observed to be thoughtful and retiring. She passed much of her time in solitude and seemed ever to prefer the companionship of her own shadow to the society of the lodge-circle.

Whenever she could leave her father's lodge she would fly to remote haunts and recesses in the woods, or sit in lonely reverie upon some high promontory of rock overlooking the lake. In such places she would often linger long, with her face turned upward, in contemplation of the air, as if she were invoking her guardian spirit and beseeching him to lighten her sadness.

But of all the leafy haunts, none drew her steps toward it so often as a forest of pines on the open shore, called Manitowok, or the Sacred Wood. It was one of those hallowed places which is the resort of the little wild men of the woods, and of the turtle spirits or fairies which delight in romantic scenes

Owing to this circumstance, its green retirement was seldom visited by Indians, who feared to fall under the influence of its mischievous inhabitants. Whenever they were compelled by stress of weather to make a landing on this part of the coast, they never failed to leave an offering of tobacco or some other token, to show that they desired to stand well with the proprietors of the fairy ground.

To this sacred spot Leelinau had made her way at an early age, gathering strange flowers and plants, which she would bring home to her parents, and relating to them all the haps and mishaps that had occurred in her rambles.

Although they discountenanced her frequent visits to the place, they were not able to restrain them, for she was of so gentle and delicate a temper that they feared to thwart her.

Her attachment to the fairy wood, therefore, grew with her years. If she wished to solicit her guardian spirits to procure pleasant dreams, or any other maiden favor, Leelinau repaired to the Manitowok. If her father remained abroad in the hunt later than usual, and it was feared that he had been overwhelmed by the tempest or had met with some other mischance, Leelinau offered up her prayers for safety at the Manitowok. It was there that she fasted, mused, and strolled.

She at length became so engrossed by the fairy pines that her parents began to suspect that some evil spirit

had enticed her to its haunts and had cast upon her
a charm which she had not the power to resist.

This belief was confirmed when, one day, her mother,
who had secretly followed her, overheard her murmuring to some unknown and invisible companion, appeals
like these:

"Spirit of the dancing leaves!" whispered Leelinau,
"hear a throbbing heart in its sadness. Spirit of the
foaming stream! visit thou my nightly pillow, shedding over it silver dreams of mountain brook and
pebbly rivulet. Spirit of the starry night! lead my
foot-prints to the blushing mis-kodeed, or where the
burning passion-flower shines with carmine hue.
Spirit of the greenwood plume!" she concluded, turning with passionate gaze to the beautiful young pines
which stood waving their green beauty over her head,
"shed on me, on Leelinau the sad, thy leafy fragrance,
such as spring unfolds from sweetest flowers, or hearts
that to each other show their inmost grief. Spirits!
hear, oh, hear a maiden's prayer!"

Day by day these strange communings with unseen
beings drew away the heart of Leelinau more and
more from the simple duties of the lodge, and she
walked among her people, melancholy and silent, like
a spirit who had visited them from another land.

The pastimes which engaged the frolic moments of
her young companions passed by her as little trivial
pageants in which she had no concern.

When the girls of the neighboring lodges assembled to play before the lodge-door at the favorite game of pappus-e-kowaun, or the block and string, Leelinau would sit vacantly by, or enter so feebly into the spirit of the play as to show that it was irksome to her.

Again, in the evening, when the young people formed a ring around the lodge, and the piepeendjigun, or leather and bone, passed rapidly from one to the other, she either handed it along without attempting to play, or if she took a part, it was with no effort to succeed.

The time of the corn-gathering had come, and the young people of the tribe were assembled in the field, busy in plucking the ripened maize. One of the girls, noted for her beauty, had found a red ear, and every one congratulated her that a brave admirer was on his way to her father's lodge. She blushed, and hiding the trophy in her bosom, thanked the Good Spirit that it was a red ear, and not a crooked, that she had found.

Presently it chanced that one who was there among the young men espied in the hands of Leelinau, who had plucked it indifferently, one of the crooked kind, and at once the word "Wa-ge-min!" was shouted aloud through the field, and the whole circle was set in a roar.

"The thief is in the corn-field!" exclaimed the young man, Iagoo by name, and famous in the tribe for his mirthful powers of story-telling; "see you not the old man stooping as he enters the field? See you not signs that he crouched as he crept in the dark? Is it not plain by this mark on the stalk that he was heavily bent in his back? Old man! be nimble, or some one will take thee while thou art taking the ear.''

These questions Iagoo accompanied with the action of one bowed with age stealthily entering the corn-field. He went on:

"See how he stoops as he breaks off the ear. Nushka! He seems for a moment to tremble. Walker, be nimble! Hooh! It is plain the old man is the thief.''

He turned suddenly where she sat in the circle, pensively regarding the crooked ear which she held in her hand, and exclaimed:

"Leelinau, the old man is thine!''

Laughter rang merrily through the corn-field, but Leelinau, casting down upon the ground the crooked ear of maize, walked pensively away.

The next morning the eldest son of a neighboring chief called at her father's lodge. He was quite advanced in years; but he enjoyed such renown in battle, and his name was so famous in the hunt, that the parents accepted him as a suitor for their daughter. They hoped that his shining qualities would draw back the thoughts of Leelinau from that spirit-land whither she seemed to have wholly directed her affections.

It was this chief's son whom Iagoo had pictured as the corn-taker, but, without objecting to his age or giving any other reason, Leelinau firmly declined his proposals. The parents ascribed the young daughter's hesitancy to maiden shyness, and paying no further heed to her refusal, fixed a day for the marriage-visit to the lodge.

The young warrior came to the lodge-door, and Leelinau refused to see him, informing her parents, at the same time, that she would never consent to the match.

It had been her custom to pass many of her hours in her favorite place of retirement under a broad-topped young pine, whose leaves whispered in every wind that blew; but most of all in that gentle murmur of the air at the evening hour, dear to lovers, when the twilight steals on.

Thither she now repaired, and, while reclining pensively against the young pine-tree, she fancied that she heard a voice addressing her. At first it was scarcely more than a sigh; presently it grew more clear, and she heard it distinctly whisper—

"Maiden! think me not a tree; but thine own dear lover; fond to be with thee in my tall and blooming strength, with the bright green nodding plume that waves above thee. Thou art leaning on my breast, Leelinau; lean forever there and be at peace. Fly from men who are false and cruel, and quit the tumult of their dusty strife for this quiet, lonely shade. Over thee I will fling my arms, fairer than the lodge's roof. I will breathe a perfume like that of flowers over thy happy evening rest. In my bark canoe I'll waft thee over the waters of the sky-blue lake. I will deck the folds of thy mantle with the sun's last rays. Come and wander with me on the mountains, a fairy free!"

Leelinau drank in with eager ear these magical words. Her heart was fixed. No warrior's son should clasp her hand. She listened in the hope to hear the airy voice speak more; but it only repeated, "Again! again!" and entirely ceased.

On the eve of the day fixed for her marriage, Leelinau decked herself in her best garments. She arranged her hair according to the fashion of her tribe and put on all of her maiden ornaments in beautiful array. With a smile, she presented herself before her parents.

"I am going," she said, "to meet my little lover, the Chieftain of the Green Plume, who is waiting for me at the Spirit Grove."

Her face was radiant with joy, and the parents, taking what she had said as her own fanciful way of expressing acquiescence in their plans, wished her good fortune in the happy meeting.

"I am going," she continued, addressing her mother as they left the lodge, "I am going from one who has watched my infancy and guarded my youth; who has given me medicine when I was sick and prepared my food when I was well. I am going from a father who has ranged the forest to procure the choicest skins for my dress and kept his lodge supplied with the best spoil of the chase. I am going from a lodge which has been my shelter from the storms of winter and my shield from the heats of summer. Farewell, my parents, farewell!''

So saying, she sped faster than any could follow her to the margin of the fairy wood, and in a moment was lost to sight.

As she had often thus withdrawn herself from the lodge, the parents were not in fear but confidently awaited her return. Hour chased hour, as the clouds of evening rolled up in the west; darkness came on, but no daughter returned. With torches they hastened to the wood, but although they lit up every dark recess and leafy gloom, their search was in vain. Leelinau was nowhere to be seen. They called aloud, in lament, upon her name, but she answered not.

Suns rose and set, but nevermore in their light did the bereaved parents' eyes behold the lost form of their beloved child. Their daughter was lost indeed. Whither she had vanished no mortal tongue could tell; although it chanced that a company of fishermen, who were spearing fish near the Siprit Grove, descried something that seemed to resemble a maiden's figure standing on the shore. As the evening was mild and the waters calm, they cautiously pulled their canoe toward land, but the slight ripple of their oars excited alarm. The figure fled in haste, but they could recognise in the shape and dress as she ascended the bank, the lost daughter, and they saw the green plumes of her fairy-lover waving over his forehead as he glided lightly through the forest of young pines.

XIV

THE WINTER SPIRIT AND HIS VISITOR

AN old man was sitting alone in his lodge by the side of a frozen stream. It was the close of winter, and his fire was almost out. He appeared very old and very desolate. His locks were white with age, and he trembled in every joint. Day after day passed in solitude, and he heard nothing but the sounds of the tempest, sweeping before it the new-fallen snow.

One day as his fire was just dying, a handsome young man approached and entered his dwelling. His cheeks were red with the blood of youth; his eyes sparkled with life; and a smile played upon his lips. He walked with a light and quick step. His forehead was bound with a wreath of sweet grass, in place of the warrior's frontlet, and he carried a bunch of flowers in his hand.

"Ah! my son," said the old man, "I am happy to see you. Come in. Come, tell me of your adventures, and what strange lands you have been to see. Let us pass the night together. I will tell you of my prowess and exploits, and what I can perform. You shall do the same, and we will amuse ourselves."

He then drew from his sack a curiously wrought

antique pipe, and having filled it with tobacco rendered mild by an admixture of certain dried leaves, he handed it to his guest. When this ceremony was attended to, they began to speak.

"I blow my breath," said the old man, "and the streams stand still. The water becomes stiff and hard as clear stone."

"I breathe," said the young man, "and flowers spring up all over the plains."

"I shake my locks," retorted the old man, "and snow covers the land. The leaves fall from the trees at my command, and my breath blows them away. The birds rise from the water and fly to a distant land. The animals hide themselves from the glance of my eye, and the very ground where I walk becomes as hard as flint."

"I shake my ringlets," rejoined the young man, "and warm showers of soft rain fall upon the earth. The plants lift up their heads out of the ground like the eyes of children glistening with delight. My voice recalls the birds. The warmth of my breath unlocks the streams. Music fills the groves wherever I walk, and all nature welcomes my approach."

At length the sun began to rise. A gentle warmth came over the place. The tongue of the old man became silent. The robin and the blue-bird began to sing on the top of the lodge. The stream began to murmur by the door, and the fragrance of growing herbs and flowers came softly on the breeze.

Daylight fully revealed to the young man the character of his entertainer. When he looked upon him he saw the visage of Peboan, the icy old Winter-Spirit. Streams began to flow from the old man's eyes. As the sun increased he grew less and less in stature, and presently he had melted completely away. Nothing remained on the place of his lodge-fire but the mis-kodeed, a small white flower with a pink border, which the young visitor, Seegwun, the Spirit of Spring, placed in the wreath upon his brow, as his first trophy in the North.

XV

THE ENCHANTED MOCCASINS

A LONG, long time ago, a little boy was living with his sister entirely alone in an uninhabited country far out in the north-west. He was called the Boy That Carries the Ball on his Back, from an idea that he possessed magical powers. This boy was in the habit of meditating alone and asking within himself whether there were other beings similar to himself and his sister on the earth.

When he grew up to manhood, he inquired of his sister whether she knew of any human beings besides themselves. She replied that she did; and that there was, at a great distance, a large village.

As soon as he heard this, he said to his sister:

"I am now a young man and very much in want of a companion."

He asked his sister to make him several pairs of moccasins. She complied with his request; and as soon as he received the moccasins, he took up his war-club and set out in quest of the distant village.

He traveled on till he came to a small wigwam, in which he discovered a very old woman sitting alone by the fire. As soon as she saw the stranger, she invited him in, and thus addressed him:

"My poor grandchild, I suppose you are one of those who seek for the distant village, from which no person has ever yet returned. Unless your guardian is more powerful than the guardians of those who have gone before you, you will share a similar fate to theirs. Be careful to provide yourself with the invisible bones those people use in the medicine-dance, for without these you cannot succeed."

After she had thus spoken, she gave him the following directions for his journey:

"When you come near to the village which you seek, you will see in the center a large lodge, in which the chief of the village, who has two daughters, resides. Before the door there is a great tree, which is smooth and without bark. On this tree, about the height of a man from the ground, is hung a small lodge, in which these two false daughters dwell. It is here that so many have been destroyed, and among them your two elder brothers. Be wise, my grandchild, and abide strictly by my directions."

The old woman then gave to the young man the bones which were to secure his success; and she informed him with great care how he was to proceed.

Placing them in his bosom, Onwee Bahmondang, or The Wearer of the Ball, continued his journey and kept eagerly on until he arrived at the village of which he was in search. Here, on gazing around, he saw both the tree and the lodge which the old woman had mentioned.

He at once bent his steps toward the tree, and approaching, endeavored to reach the suspended lodge. But all his efforts were in vain; for as often as he attempted to reach it, the tree began to tremble, and it soon shot up so that the lodge could hardly be perceived.

He bethought him of his guardian spirit, so invoking his aid and changing himself into a squirrel, he mounted nimbly up again, in the hope that the lodge would not now escape him. But to his disappointment away shot the lodge, climb as briskly as he might.

Panting and out of breath, he at last remembered the instructions of the old woman. Drawing from his bosom one of the bones, he thrust it into the trunk of the tree and rested himself upon it to be ready to start again.

As often as he wearied of climbing, for even a squirrel cannot climb forever, he repeated the little ceremony of the bones; but whenever he came near the lodge and put forth his hand to touch it, the tree would shoot up as before and carry the lodge up far beyond his reach.

At length the bones being all gone, and the lodge well-nigh out of sight, he began to despair, for the earth, too, had long since vanished entirely from his view.

Summoning his whole heart, he resolved to try once

more. On and up he went, but as soon as he put forth his hand to touch it, the tree again shook, and away went the lodge.

One more endeavor, brave Onwee, and in he goes; for having now reached the arch of heaven, the fly-away lodge could go no higher.

Onwee entered with a fearless step and beheld the two wicked sisters sitting opposite each other. He asked their names. The one on his left hand called herself Azhabee, and the one on the right, Negahna-bee.

After talking with them a little while, he discovered that whenever he addressed the one on his left hand, the tree would tremble as before and settle down to its former place; but when he addressed the one on his right hand, it would again shoot upward.

When he thus perceived that by addressing the one on his left hand the tree would descend, he continued to do so until it had again settled down to its place near the earth. Then seizing his war-club, he said to the sisters:

"You who have caused the death of so many of my brethren I will now put an end to, and thus have revenge for those you have destroyed."

As he spoke this he raised the club and with one blow laid the two wicked women dead at his feet.

Onwee then descended, and learned that these sisters had a brother living with their father, who had shared in the spoils of all such as the wicked sisters had betrayed. This youth would now pursue him for having put an end to their wicked profits, so Onwee set off at random, not knowing whither he went.

The father, coming in the evening to visit the lodge of his daughters, discovered what had happened. He immediately sent word to his son that the sisters had been slain, and that there were no more spoils to be had. Now this news greatly inflamed the brother's temper, especially the woful announcement at the end. He was chafing and half beside himself with rage.

"Oh," he cried. "The person who has done this must be that Boy That Carries the Ball on his Back. I know his mode of going about his business, and since he would not allow himself to be killed by my sisters, he shall have the honor of dying by my hand. I will pursue him and have revenge."

"It is well, my son," replied the father; "the spirit of your life grant you success. But I counsel you to be wary in the pursuit. Onwee Bahmondang is a cunning youth. It is a strong spirit who has put him on to do this injury to us, and he will try to deceive you in every way. Above all, avoid tasting food till you succeed; for if you break your fast before you see his blood, your power will be destroyed."

The son took this fatherly advice all in good part, except that portion which enjoined upon him to abstain from staying his stomach; over that command he made a number of wry faces, for the brother of the two wicked sisters had, among numerous noble gifts,

a very noble appetite. Nevertheless, he took up his
weapons and departed at the top of his speed in pursuit of Onwee Bahmondang.

Onwee, finding that he was closely followed, climbed
up into one of the tallest sycamore-trees and shot
forth the magic arrows with which he had provided
himself.

Seeing that his pursuer was not turned back by his
arrows, Onwee renewed his flight; and when he found
himself hard pressed and his enemy close behind him,
he transformed himself into the skeleton of a moose
that had been killed many moons before. He then
remembered the moccasins which his sister had given
him, and taking a pair of them, he placed them near
the skeleton.

"Go," said he to them, "to the end of the earth."

The moccasins then left him, and their tracks remained.

The angry brother at length came to the skeleton
of the moose. When he perceived that the track he
had been long pursuing did not stop there, he continued to follow it up till he arrived at the end of the
earth, where, for all his trouble, he found only a pair
of moccasins.

Vexed that he had been outwitted by following a
pair of moccasins instead of their owner, he com-
plained bitterly, resolving not to give up his revenge
and to be more wary in the future.

He then called to mind the skeleton he had met with

on his way, and concluded that it must be the object of his search.

So the brother retraced his steps toward the skeleton, but to his surprise it had disappeared, and the tracks of the Wearer of the Ball were in another direction. He now became faint with hunger, and lost heart; but when he remembered the blood of his sisters, and that he should not be allowed to enjoy a meal, or so much as a mouthful, until he had put an end to Onwee Bahmondang, he plucked up his spirits and determined again to pursue.

Onwee, finding that he was closely followed and that the hungry brother was approaching very fast, changed himself into a very old man, with two daughters. They lived in a large lodge in the center of a beautiful garden, which was filled with everything that could delight the eye or was pleasant to the taste. He made himself appear so very old as to be unable to leave his lodge and to require his daughters to bring him food and wait on him, as though he had been a mere child. The garden also had the appearance of old age, with its ancient bushes and hanging branches and decrepit vines loitering lazily about in the sun.

Meanwhile the brother kept on until he was nearly starved and ready to sink to the earth. He exclaimed, with a long-drawn and most mournful sigh:

"Oh! I will forget the blood of my sisters, for I am starving. Oh! oh!"

But again he thought of the blood of his sisters,

and what a fine appetite he would have if he should ever be allowed to eat anything again, and once more he resolved to pursue and to be content with nothing short of the amplest revenge.

He pushed on till he came to the beautiful garden. He advanced toward the lodge.

As soon as the fairy daughters perceived him, they ran and told their father that a stranger approached.

Their father replied, "Invite him in, my children, invite him in."

They did so promptly, and, by the command of their father, they boiled some corn and prepared several other palatable dishes. The savor was most delicious to the nostrils of the hungry brother, who had not the least suspicion of the sport that was going on at his expense.

He was faint and weary with travel, and he felt that he could endure fasting no longer; for his appetite was terribly inflamed by the sight of the choice food that was steaming before him.

He fell to and partook heartily of the meal; and by so doing he was overcome and lost his right of revenge. All at once he forgot the blood of his sisters, and even the village of his nativity; he also forgot his father's lodge, and his whole past life. He ate so keenly, and came and went to the choice dishes so often, that drowsiness at length overpowered him, and he soon fell into a profound sleep.

Onwee Bahmondang watched his opportunity, and

as soon as he saw that the false brother's sleep was
sound, he resumed his youthful form and sent off the
two fairy daughters and the old garden. Then drawing the magic-ball from his back, and turning it into
a great war-club, he fetched the slumbering brother
a mighty blow, which sent him away too. And thus
did Onwee Bahmondang vindicate his title as The
Wearer of the Ball.

Such was the great force and weight of the club with
which he had despatched the brother of the two wicked
women that it swung Onwee straight around, and he
found himself in a large village, surrounded by a great
crowd of people. At the door of a beautiful lodge
stood his sister, smiling, and ready to invite him in.
Onwee entered, and hanging up his war-club and the
enchanted moccasins, he rested from his labors and
smoked his evening pipe, with the admiration and ap-
proval of the whole world.

With one exception only, Onwee Bahmondang had
the hearty praises of all the people.

Now it happened that there lived in this same village an envious and boastful fellow, who had been
once a chief. Always coming home badly whipped, he
had been put out of office, and now spent his time about
the place, proclaiming certain great things which he
had in his eye and which he meant to do—one of these
days.

This man's name was Ko-ko, the Owl; and hearing
much of the wonderful achievements of the Wearer

of the Ball, Ko-ko put on a big look and announced that he was going to do something extraordinary himself.

Onwee Bahmondang, he said, had not half done his work, and he, Ko-ko, meant to go on the ground and finish it up as it should be.

He began by procuring an oak ball, which he thrust down his back, and, confident in its magical powers, he, too, called himself The Wearer of the Ball. In fact it was the self-same ball that Onwee had employed, except that the magic had entirely gone out of it. Coming by night in the shadow of Onwee's lodge, this bad fellow thrust his arm in at the door and stealthily possessed himself of the enchanted moccasins. He would have taken away Onwee's war-club, too, if he could have carried it; but although he was twice the size and girth of Onwee, he had not the strength to lift it; so he borrowed a club from an old chief, who was purblind and mistook Ko-ko for his brother, who was a brave man. This accomplished, Ko-ko raised a terrible tumult with his voice and a great dust with his heels, and set out.

He had traveled all day, when he came to a small wigwam, on looking into which he discovered a very old woman sitting alone by the fire; just as Onwee had before.

This is the wigwam, said Ko-ko, and this is the old woman.

"What are you looking for?" asked the old woman.

"I want to find the lodge with the wicked young women in it, those who slay travelers and steal their trappings," answered Ko-ko.

"You mean the two young women who lived in the flying lodge?" asked the old woman.

"The same," answered Ko-ko. "I am going to kill them."

With this he gave a great flourish with his borrowed club, and looked as desperate and murderous as he could.

"They were slain yesterday by The Wearer of the Ball," said the old woman.

Ko-ko looked around for the door in a very owlish way and heaved a short hem from his chest. Then he acknowledged that he had heard something to that effect down in one of the villages.

"But there's the brother. I'll have a chance at him," said Ko-ko.

"He is dead, too," said the old woman.

"Is there then nobody left for me to kill?" cried Ko-ko. "Must I then go back without any blood upon my hands?"

He made as if he could shed tears over his sad mishap.

"The father is still living; and you will find him in the lodge, if you have a mind to call on him. He would like to see the Owl," the old woman added.

"He shall," replied Ko-ko. "Have you any bones

about the house; for I suppose I shall have to climb that tree."

"Oh, yes; plenty," answered the old woman. "You can have as many as you want."

And she gave him a handful of fish-bones, which Ko-ko thrust into his bosom, taking them to be the Invisible Tallies which had helped Onwee Bahmondang in climbing the magical tree.

"Thank you," said Ko-ko, taking up his club and striding toward the door.

"Will you not have a little advice," said the old woman. "This is a dangerous business you are going on."

Ko-ko turned about and laughed to scorn the proposal. Then putting forth his right foot from the lodge first, an observance in which he had great hopes, he started for the lodge of the wicked father.

Ko-ko ran very fast, as if he feared he should lose the chance of massacring any member of the wicked family, and soon came in sight of the lodge hanging upon the tree.

He then slackened his pace and crept forward with a wary eye, lest somebody might chance to be looking out at the door. All was still up there, however, and Ko-ko clasped the tree and began to climb.

Away went the lodge, and up went Ko-ko, puffing and panting, after it. And it was not a great while before the Owl had puffed and panted away all the wind he had to spare; and yet the lodge kept flying aloft, higher, higher. What was to be done!

Ko-ko, of course, bethought him of the bones, for that was just what, as he knew, had occurred to Onwee Bahmondang under the like circumstances.

He had the bones in his bosom; but first it was necessary for him to be a squirrel. He immediately called on several guardian spirits whom he knew of by name, and requested them to convert him into a squirrel. But not one of all of them seemed to pay the slightest attention to his request; for there he hung, the same heavy-limbed, big-headed, be-clubbed, and be-blanketed Ko-ko as ever.

He then desired that they would turn him into an opossum; an application which met with the same luck as the previous one. After this he petitioned to be a wolf, a gophir, a dog, or a bear—if they would be so obliging. The guardian spirits were either all deaf, or indifferent to his wishes, or absent on some other business.

Ko-ko, in spite of all his begging and supplication and beseeching, was obliged to be still Ko-ko.

"However, the bones are good," he said to himself. "I shall get a nice rest, at any rate, if I am forced to climb as I am."

With this he drew out one of the bones from his bosom, and shouting aloud, "Ho! ho! who is there?" he thrust it into the trunk of the tree and would have indulged himself in a rest; but being no more than a

common fish-bone, without the slightest savor of
magic in it, it snapped with Ko-ko, who came tumbling
down, with the door of the lodge, which he had shaken
loose, rattling after him.

"Ho! ho! who is there?" cried the wicked father,
making his appearance at the opening and looking
down.

"It is I, Onwee Bahmondang!" cried Ko-ko, thinking to frighten the wicked father.

"Ah! it is you, is it? I will be there presently,"
called the old man. "Do not be in haste to go
away!"

Ko-ko, observing that the old man was in earnest,
scrambled up from the ground and set off promptly
at his highest rate of speed.

When he looked back and saw that the wicked father was gaining upon him, Ko-ko mounted a tree,
as had Onwee Bahmondang before. Then he fired off
a number of arrows, but as they were no more than
common arrows, he got nothing by it, but was obliged
to descend and run again for his life.

As he hurried on he encountered the skeleton of a
moose, into which he would have transformed himself; but not having the slightest confidence in any
one of all the guardians who should have helped him,
he passed on.

The wicked father was hot in pursuit and Ko-ko
was suffering terribly for lack of wind, when luckily
he remembered the enchanted moccasins. He would

not send them to the end of the earth, as had Onwee Bahmondang.

"I will improve on that dull fellow," said Ko-ko. "I will put them on myself."

Accordingly, Ko-ko had just time to draw on the moccasins when the wicked father came in sight.

"Go now!" cried Ko-ko, giving orders to the enchanted moccasins; and go they did. But to the astonishment of the Owl, they turned immediately about in the way in which the wicked father was furiously approaching.

"The other way! the other way!" cried Ko-ko.

Cry as loud as he would, the enchanted moccasins would keep on in their own course; and before he could shake himself out of them, they had run him directly into the face of the wicked father.

"What do you mean, you Owl?" cried the wicked father, falling upon Ko-ko with a huge club, and counting his ribs at every stroke.

"I cannot help it, good man," answered Ko-ko. "I tried my best—"

Ko-ko would have gone the other way, but the enchanted moccasins kept hurrying him forward.

"Stand off, will you?" cried the old man.

By this time the moccasins were taking him past, allowing the wicked father chance to bestow no more than five-and-twenty more blows upon Ko-ko.

"Stop!" cried the old man again. "You are running away. Ho! ho! you are a coward!"

"I am not, good man," answered Ko-ko, carried away by the magical shoes, "I assure you." But ere he could finish his avowal, the moccasins had hurried him out of sight.

"At any rate, I shall soon be home at this speed," said Ko-ko to himself.

The moccasins seemed to know his thoughts; for just then they gave a sudden leap, slipped away from his feet, and left the Owl flat upon his back! while they glided home by themselves to the lodge of Onwee Bahmondang, where they belonged.

A party of hunters passing that way after several days, found Ko-ko sitting among the bushes, looking greatly bewildered. When they inquired of him how he had succeeded with the wicked father at the lodge, he answered that he had demolished the whole establishment, but that his name was not Ko-ko, but Onwee Bahmondang; saying which, he ran away into the woods, and was never seen more.

XVI

THE WEENDIGOES AND THE BONE-DWARF

THERE once lived a man and his wife and their son in a lonely forest. The father went forth every day, according to the custom of the Indians, to hunt for food to supply his family.

One day while he was absent, his wife, on going out of the lodge, looked toward the lake that was near and saw a very large man walking on the water, coming fast toward the lodge. He was already so near that she could not escape by flight, even if she had wished to.

"What shall I say to the monster?" she thought to herself.

As he advanced rapidly, she ran in, and taking the hand of her son, a boy of three or four years old, she led him out. Speaking very loud, "See, my son," she said, "your grandfather"; and then added in a tone of appeal and supplication, "he will have pity on us."

The giant approached and said, with a loud ha! ha! "Yes, my son"; and added, addressing the woman, "Have you anything to eat?"

By good luck the lodge was well supplied with meats of various kinds. The woman thought to please him by handing him these, which were savory and carefully prepared. But he pushed them away in disgust, saying, "I smell fire"; and not waiting to be invited, he seized upon the carcass of a deer which lay by the door and despatched it almost without stopping to take breath.

When the hunter came home he was surprised to see the monster, he was so very frightful. He had again brought a deer, which he had no sooner put down than the cannibal seized it, tore it in pieces, and devoured it as though he had been fasting for a week. The hunter looked on in fear and astonishment, and in a whisper he told his wife that he was afraid for their lives, as this monster was one of those monsters whom Indians call Weendigoes. He did not even dare to speak to him, nor did the cannibal say a word, but as soon as he had finished his meal, stretched himself down and fell asleep.

In the evening the Weendigo told the people that he should go out a-hunting; and he strided away toward the North. Toward morning he returned, all besmeared with blood, but he did not make known where he had been or of what kind of game he had been in quest; but the hunter and his wife had dreadful suspicions of the sport in which he had been engaged. Withal his hunger did not seem to be staid, for he took up the deer which the hunter had brought in and devoured it eagerly, leaving the family to make their meal of the dried meats which had been reserved in the lodge.

In this manner the Weendigo and the hunter's family lived for some time, and it surprised them that the monster did not attempt their lives; he never slept at night, but always went out and returned by the break of day stained with blood and looking very wild and famished. When there was no deer to be had wherewith to finish his repast, he said nothing. In truth he was always still and gloomy, and he seldom spoke to any of them; when he did, his discourse was chiefly addressed to the boy.

One evening, after he had thus sojourned with them for many weeks, he informed the hunter that the time had now arrived for him to take his leave, but that before doing so, he would give him a charm that would bring good luck to his lodge. He presented to him two arrows, and thanking the hunter and his wife for their kindness, the Weendigo departed, saying, as he left them, that he had all the world to travel over.

The hunter and his wife were happy when he was gone, for they had looked every moment to have been devoured by him. Then they tried the arrows, which never failed to bring down whatever they were aimed at.

So they lived on, prosperous and contented, for a year. One day when the hunter was absent, his wife, going out of the lodge, saw something like a black cloud approaching.

She looked until it came near, when she perceived that it was another Weendigo, or Giant Cannibal,

Remembering the good conduct of the other, she had no fear of this one, and asked him to look into the lodge.

He did so; but finding after he had glared around that there was no food at hand, he grew very wroth, and being sorely disappointed, he took the lodge and threw it to the winds. He seemed hardly at first to notice the woman in his anger; but presently he cast a fierce glance upon her, and seizing her by the waist, in spite of her cries and entreaties, he bore her off. To the little son, who ran to and fro lamenting, he paid no heed.

When the hunter returned from the forest at night-fall, he was amazed. His lodge was gone, and he saw his son sitting near the spot where it had stood, shedding tears. The son pointed in the direction the Weendigo had taken, and as the father hurried along he found the bones of his wife strewn upon the ground.

The hunter blackened his face and vowed in his heart that he would have revenge. He built another lodge, and gathering together the bones of his wife, he placed them in the hollow part of a dry tree.

He left his boy to take care of the lodge while he was absent. Then he went hunting and roaming about from place to place, striving to forget his misfortune, and always searching for the wicked Weendigo.

One morning he had been gone but a little while, when his son shot his arrows out through the top of the lodge; running out to look for them, he could find them nowhere. The boy had been trying his luck, and he was puzzled that he had shot his shafts entirely out of sight.

His father made him more arrows, and when he was again left alone, he shot one of them out; but although he looked as sharply as he could toward the spot where it fell, and ran thither at once, he could not find it. He shot another, which was lost in the same way. Returning to the lodge to replenish his quiver, he happened to espy one of the lucky arrows which the first Weendigo had given to his father, hanging upon the side of the lodge. He reached up, and having secured it, he shot it out at the opening. Immediately running out to find where it fell, he was surprised to see a beautiful boy just in the act of taking it up and hurrying away with it to a large tree. There he disappeared.

The hunter's son followed, and having come to the tree, beheld the face of the boy looking out through an opening in the hollow part.

"Ha! ha!" he said, "my friend, come out and play with me." And he urged the boy till he consented. They played and shot their arrows by turns.

Suddenly the young boy said, "Your father is coming. We must stop. Promise me that you will not tell him."

The hunter's son promised, and the other disappeared in the tree.

When the hunter returned from the chase, his son

sat demurely by the fire. In the course of the evening he asked his father to make him a new bow; and when he was questioned as to the use he could find for two bows, he answered that one might break or get lost.

The father, pleased at his son's diligence in the practise of the bow, made him the new weapon; and the next day, as soon as his father had gone away, the boy ran to the hollow tree and invited his little friend to come out and play, at the same time presenting to him the new bow. They went and played in the lodge together, and in their sport they raised the ashes all over it.

Suddenly again the youngest said, "Your father is coming, I must leave."

He again exacted a promise of secrecy and went back to his tree. The eldest took his seat near the fire.

When the hunter came in he was surprised to see the ashes scattered about. "Why, my son," he said, "you must have played very hard to-day to raise such a dust all alone."

"Yes," the boy answered, "I was very lonesome, and I ran round and round—that is the cause of it."

The next day the hunter made ready for the chase as usual. The boy said:

"Father, try and hunt all day, and see what you can kill."

He had no sooner set out than the boy called his

friend, and they played and chased each other round the lodge. They had great delight in each other's company and made merry by the hour. The hunter was again returning, and came to a rising ground which caught the winds as they passed, when he heard his son laughing and making a noise; but the sounds as they reached him on the hill-top, seemed as if they arose from two persons playing.

At the same time the younger boy stopped, and after saying, "Your father is coming," stole away under cover of the high grass to his hollow tree, which was not far off.

The hunter, on entering, found his son sitting by the fire, very quiet and unconcerned, although he saw that all the articles of the lodge were lying thrown about in all directions.

"Why, my son," he said, "you must play very hard every day; and what is it that you do, all alone, to throw the lodge in such confusion?"

The boy again had his excuse. "Father," he answered, "I play in this manner: I chase and drag my blanket around the lodge, and that is the reason you see the ashes spread about."

The hunter was not satisfied until his son had shown him how he played with the blanket, which he did so adroitly as to set his father laughing and at last drive him out of the lodge with the great clouds of ashes that he raised.

The next morning the boy renewed his request that

his father should be absent all day, and see if he could not kill two deer. The hunter thought this a strange desire on the part of his son, but as he had always humored the boy, he went into the forest as usual, bent on accomplishing his wish, if he could.

As soon as he was out of sight, his son hastened to his young companion at the tree, and they continued their sports.

The father on nearing his home in the evening again heard the sounds of play and laughter; and as the wind brought them straight to his ear, he was now certain that there were two voices.

The boy from the tree had no more than time to escape, when the hunter entered and found his son sitting as usual near the fire. When he cast his eyes around, he saw that the lodge was in greater confusion than before.

"My son," he said, "you must be very foolish to play so when alone. But, tell me, my son; I heard two voices, I am sure," and he looked closely on the prints of the footsteps in the ashes. "True," he continued, "here is the print of a foot which is smaller than yours," and he was now satisfied that his suspicions were well founded, and that some very young person had been the companion of his son during his absence.

The boy could not now refuse to tell his father what had happened.

"Father," he said, "I found a boy in the hollow of

that tree near the lodge, where you placed my mother's bones.''

Strange thoughts came over the mind of the hunter; did his wife live again in this beautiful child?

Fearful of disturbing the dead, he did not dare to visit the place where he had deposited her remains.

He, however, engaged his son to entice the boy to a dead tree by the edge of a wood, where they could kill many flying-squirrels by setting it on fire. He said that he would conceal himself near-by and take the boy.

The next day the hunter accordingly went into the woods, and his son, calling the boy from the tree, urged him to go with him to kill the squirrels. The boy objected that the father was near, but he was at length prevailed on to go, and after they had fired the tree, and while they were busy killing or taking the squirrels, the hunter suddenly made his appearance and clasped the strange boy in his arms.

''Kago, kago, don't, don't,'' cried the child. ''You will tear my clothes!'' For he was clad in a fine apparel, which shone as if it had been made of a beautiful transparent skin. The father reassured him by every means in his power.

By constant kindness and gentle words the boy was reconciled to remain with them; but chiefly by the presence of his young friend, the hunter's son, to whom he was fondly attached. The children were never parted from each other; and when the hunter looked upon the strange boy, he seemed to see living in him the better spirit of his lost wife. He was thankful to the Great Spirit for this act of goodness, and in his heart he felt assured that in time the boy would show great virtue and in some way avenge him on the wicked Weendigo who had destroyed the companion of his lodge.

The hunter grew at ease in his spirit and gave all of the time he could spare from the chase to the society of the two children; but what affected him most, both of his sons, although they were well-formed and beautiful, grew no more in stature but remained children still. Every day they resembled each other more and more, and they never ceased to sport and divert themselves in the innocent ways of childhood.

One day the hunter had gone abroad with his bow and arrows, leaving behind in the lodge, at the request of the strange boy, one of the two shafts which the friendly Weendigo had given to him.

When he returned, what were his surprise and joy to see stretched dead by his lodge-door the black giant who had slain his wife. He had been stricken down by the magic shaft in the hands of the little stranger from the tree; and ever after the boy, or the Bone-Dwarf as he was called, was the guardian and good genius of the lodge. No evil spirit, giant, or Weendigo, ever again dared approach it to mar their peace.

XVII

THE FIRE-PLUME

WASSAMO was living with his parents on the shore of a large bay far out in the north-east.

One day, when the season had commenced for fish to be plenty, the mother of Wassamo said to him:

"My son, I wish you would go to yonder point and see if you cannot procure me some fish; and ask your cousin to accompany you."

Wassamo did so. He set out with his cousin, and in the course of the afternoon they arrived at the fishing-ground.

The cousin, being the elder, attended to the nets. When these were set in the lake, the youths encamped near-by, using the bark of the birch for a lodge to shelter them through the night.

They lit a fire, and while they sat conversing with each other, the moon arose. Not a breath of wind disturbed the smooth surface of the lake. Not a cloud was seen. Wassamo looked out on the water toward their nets, and he saw that the little black spots, which were no other than the floats, had disappeared.

"Netawis," he said, "let us visit our nets; perhaps we are fortunate."

When they drew up the nets they were rejoiced to

see the meshes shining white, all over, with the glittering prey. They landed in fine spirits, and put away their canoe in safety from the winds.

"Wassamo," said the cousin, "you cook that we may eat."

Wassamo set about the work at once and soon had his great kettle swung upon its branch, while the cousin lay at his ease upon the other side of the fire.

"Cousin," said Wassamo, "tell me stories or sing me some love-songs."

The cousin obeyed, and sang his plaintive songs, frequently breaking off in the midst of a mournful chant to recite a mirthful story, then in the midst of Wassamo's laughter returning to the plaintive ditty —just as it suited his fancy; for Netawis was gay of spirit and shifted his humor faster than the fleecy clouds that appeared and disappeared in the night-sky over their heads. In this changeful pastime the cousin ran his length and then fell away into a silvery sleep, murmuring parts of his song or story, while the moon glided through the branches and gilded his face as though she were enamored of his fair looks.

Wassamo in the meanwhile had lost the sound of his cousin's voice in the rich simmer of the kettle; and when its music pleased his ear the most, as announcing that the fish were handsomely cooked, he lifted the kettle from the fire. He spoke to his cousin, but he received no answer.

He went on with his housekeeping alone and took

the wooden ladle and skimmed the kettle neatly, for
the fish were very plump and fat. But he had a torch
of twisted bark in one hand to give light, and when he
came to take out the fish, there was no one to have
charge of the torch.

The cousin was so happy in his sleep, with the silver moon kissing his cheeks, that Wassamo had not the
heart to call him up.

Binding his girdle upon his brow, in this he thrust
the torch and went forward to prepare the evening
meal with the light dancing through the green leaves
at every turn of his head.

He again spoke to his cousin, but gently, to learn
whether he was in truth asleep. The cousin mur-
mured, but made no reply; and Wassamo stepped
softly about with the dancing fire-plume lighting up
the gloom of the forest at every turn he made.

Suddenly he heard a laugh. It was double, or the
one must be the perfect echo of the other. To Wassamo there appeared to be two persons at no great
distance.

"Cousin," said Wassamo, "some person is near us.
I hear a laugh; awake and let us look out!"

The cousin made no answer.

Again Wassamo heard the laughter in mirthful
repetition, like the ripple of the water-brook upon the
shining pebbles of the stream. Peering out as far as
the line of the torchlight pierced into the darkness, he
beheld two beautiful young maidens smiling on him.

Their countenances appeared to be perfectly white, like the fresh snow.

He crouched down and pushed his cousin, saying in a low voice, "Awake! awake! here are two young women."

But he received no answer. His cousin seemed lost to all earthly sense and sound; for he lay unmoved, smiling, in the calm light of the moon. Wassamo started up alone and glided toward the strange maidens.

As he approached them he was more and more enraptured with their beauty; but just as he was about to speak to them, he suddenly fell to the earth, and they all three vanished together. The moon shone where they had just stood, but saw them not. Only a gentle sound of music and soft voices accompanied their vanishing, and this wakened the cousin.

As Netawis opened his eyes in a dreamy way, he saw the kettle near him. Some of the fish, he observed, were in the bowl. The fire flickered and made light and shadow; but nowhere was Wassamo to be seen. He waited, and waited again, in the expectation that Wassamo would appear.

"Perhaps," thought the cousin, "he is gone out again to visit the nets."

He looked off that way, but the canoe still lay close by the rock at the shore. He searched and found footsteps in the ashes, and out upon the green ground a little distance, and then they were utterly lost.

He was now greatly troubled in spirit, and he called aloud, "Wassamo! cousin! cousin!" but there was no answer to his call. He called again in his sorrow, louder and louder, "Wassamo! Wassamo! cousin! cousin! whither are you gone?" But no answer came to his voice of wailing. He started for the edge of the woods, crying as he ran, "My cousin!" and "Oh, my cousin!"

Hither and thither through the forest he sped with all his fleetness of foot and quickness of spirit; and when at last he found that no voice would answer him, he burst into tears and sobbed aloud.

He returned to the fire and sat down. He mused upon the absence of Wassamo with a sorely troubled heart. "He may have been playing me a trick," he thought; but it was full time that the trick should be at an end, and Wassamo returned not. The cousin cherished other hopes, but they all died away in the morning light, when he found himself alone by the hunting-fire.

"How shall I answer to his friends for Wassamo?" thought the cousin. "Although his parents are my kindred and are well assured that their son is my bosom-friend, will they receive that belief in the place of him who is lost? No, no; they will say that I have slain him, and they will require blood for blood. Oh! my cousin, whither are you gone?"

He would have rested to restore his mind to its peace, but he could not sleep; and without further

regard to net or canoe, he set off for the village, running all the way.

As they saw him approaching at such speed and
alone, they said, "Some accident has happened."

When he had come into the village, he told them
how Wassamo had disappeared. He stated all the
circumstances. He kept nothing to himself. He declared all that he knew.

Some said, "He has killed him in the dark." Others
said, "It is impossible; they were like brothers; they
would have fallen for each other. It cannot be."

At the cousin's request, many of the men visited
the fish-fire. There were no marks of blood. No
hasty steps were there to show that any conflict or
struggle had occurred. Every leaf on every tree was
in its place; and they saw, as the cousin had seen,
that the foot-prints of Wassamo stopped in the wood,
as if he had gone no farther upon the earth but had
ascended into the air.

They returned to the village, and no man was the
wiser as to the strange and sudden vanishing of Wassamo. None ever looked to see him more; only the
parents, who still hoped and awaited their son's return.

The spring, with all its blossoms and its delicate
newness of life, came among them; the Indians assembled from all the country round to celebrate their
spring feast.

Among them came the sad cousin of Wassamo. He

was pale and thin as the shadow of the shaft that flies. The pain of his mind had changed his features, and wherever he turned his eyes, they were dazzled with the sight of the red blood of his friend.

The parents of Wassamo, far gone in despair and weary with watching for his return, now demanded the life of Netawis. The village was stirred to its very heart by their loud lamentings; and after a struggle of pity, they decided to give the young man's life to the parents. They said that they had waited long enough. A day was appointed on which the cousin was to yield his life for his friend's.

He was a brave youth, and they bound him only by his word to be ready at the appointed hour. He said that he was not afraid to die; for he was innocent of the great wrong they laid to his charge.

A day or two before the time set to take his life, he wandered sadly along the shore of the lake. He looked at the glassy water, and more than once the thought to end his griefs by casting himself in its depths came upon him with such sudden force that only by severe self-control was he able to turn his steps in another direction. He reflected—

"They will say that I was guilty if I take my own life. No. I will give them my blood for that of my cousin."

He walked on with slow steps, but he found no comfort, turn where he would; the sweet songs of the forest jarred upon his ear; the beauty of the blue sky pained his sight; and the soft green earth, as he trod upon it, seemed harsh to his foot and sent a pang through every nerve.

"Oh, where is my cousin!" he kept saying to himself.

Meanwhile, when Wassamo fell senseless before the two young women in the wood, he lost all knowledge of himself until he awakened in a distant scene. He heard persons conversing. One spoke in a tone of command, saying:

"Foolish ones, is this the way that you rove about at nights without our knowledge? Put that person you have brought on that couch of yours, and do not let him lie upon the ground."

Wassamo felt himself moved, he knew not how, and placed upon a couch. Some time after, the spell seemed to be a little lightened, and on opening his eyes, he was surprised to find that he was lying in a spacious and shining lodge extending as far as the eye could reach. One spoke to him and said:

"Stranger, awake, and take something wherewith to refresh yourself."

He obeyed the command and sat up. On either side of the lodge he beheld rows of people seated in orderly array. At a distance he could see two stately persons, who looked rather more in years than the others, and who appeared to exact obedience from all around them. One of them, whom he heard addressed as the Old Spirit-man, spoke to Wassamo.

"My son," said he, "know it was those foolish maidens who brought you hither. They saw you at the fishing-ground. When you attempted to approach them you fell senseless, and at the same moment they transported you to this place. You are now under the earth. But be at ease. We will make your stay with us pleasant. I am the Guardian Spirit of the Sand Mountains. They are my charge. I pile them up and blow them about and do whatever I will with them. It keeps me very busy, but I am hale for my age, and I love to be employed. I have often wished to get one of your race to marry among us. If you can make up your mind to remain, I will give you one of my daughters—the one who smiled on you first the night you were brought away from your parents and friends."

Wassamo dropped his head and made no answer. The thought that he should behold his kindred no more made him sad.

He was silent, and the Old Spirit continued: "Your wants will all be supplied; but you must be careful not to stray far from the lodge. I am afraid of that Spirit who rules all islands lying in the lakes. He is my bitter enemy, for I have refused him my daughter in marriage; and when he learns that you are a member of my family, he will seek to harm you. There is my daughter," added the Old Spirit, pointing toward her. "Take her. She shall be your wife."

Forthwith Wassamo and the Old Spirit's daughter

sat near each other in the lodge, and they were man and wife.

One evening the Old Spirit came in after a busy day's work out among the sand-hills, in the course of which he had blown them all out of shape with great gusts of wind, strewn them about in a thousand directions and brought them back and piled them up in all sorts of misshapen heaps.

At the close of this busy day, when the Old Spirit came in very much out of breath, he said to Wassamo:

"Son-in-law, I am in want of tobacco. None grows about this dry place of mine. You shall return to your people and procure me a supply. It is seldom that the few who pass these sand-hills offer me a piece of tobacco—it is a rare plant in these parts—but when they do, it immediately comes to me. Just so," he added, putting his hand out of the side of the lodge and drawing in several pieces of tobacco. Some one passing at that moment had offered it as a fee to the Old Spirit, to keep the sand-hills from blowing about till they had got by.

Other gifts besides tobacco came in the same way to the side of the lodge—sometimes a whole bear, then a wampum-robe, then a string of birds—and the Sand-Spirits altogether led an easy life; for they were not at the trouble to hunt or clothe themselves; and whenever the housekeeping began to fall short, nothing would happen but a wonderful storm of dust, all the sand-hills being straightway put in an uproar, and the contributions would at once begin to pour in at the side windows of the lodge, till all wants were supplied.

After Wassamo had been among these curious people several months, the old Sand-Spirit said to him:

"Son-in-law, you must not be surprised at what you will see next; for since you have been with us you have never known us to go to sleep. It has been summer, when the sun never sets here where we live. But now, what you call winter is coming on. You will soon see us lie down, and we shall not rise again till the spring. Take my advice. Do not leave the lodge. I have sure knowledge that that knavish Island Spirit is on the prowl, and as he has command of a particular kind of storm, which comes from the south-west, he only waits his opportunity to catch you abroad and do you mischief. Try and amuse yourself. That cupboard," pointing to a corner of the lodge, "is never empty; for it is there that all the offerings are handed in while we are asleep. It is never empty, and—"

But ere the old Sand-Spirit could utter another word, a loud rattling of thunder was heard, and instantly not only the Old Spirit but every one of his family vanished out of sight.

When the storm had passed by, they all reappeared in the lodge. This sudden vanishing and reappearance occurred at every tempest.

"You are surprised," said the Old Spirit, "to see us disappear when it thunders. The reason is this:

that noise which you fancy is thunder is our enemy
the Island Spirit hallooing on his way home from the
hunt. We get out of sight that we may escape the
necessity of asking him to come in and share our evening meal. We are not afraid of him, not in the
least."

Just then it chanced to thunder again, and Wassamo observed that his father-in-law made extraordinary despatch to conceal himself, although no stranger was in view, at all resembling in any way the
Island Spirit.

Shortly after this the season of sleep began, and one
by one they laid themselves down to the long slumber.

The Old Spirit was the last to drop away; and before he yielded, he went forth and had his last sport
with the sand-hills. He so tossed and vexed the poor
hills, scattered them to and fro, and whirled them up
in the air and far over the land, that it was days and
days before they got back to anything like their natural shape.

While his relations were enjoying this long sleep,
Wassamo amused himself as best he could. The cupboard never failed him once; for visit it when he
would, he always found a fresh supply of game and
every other dainty which his heart desired.

But his chief pastime was to listen to the voices
of the travelers who passed by the window at the side
of the lodge, where they made their requests for comfortable weather and an easy journey.

These were often mingled with loud complainings, such as "Ho! how the sand jumps about!" "Take away that hill!" "I am lost!" "Old Sand-Spirit, where are you? Help this way!" which indicated that such as were journeying through the hills had their own troubles to encounter.

As the spring-light of the first day of spring shone into the lodge, the whole family arose and went about the affairs of the day as though they had been slumbering only for a single night. The rest seemed to have done the Old Spirit much good, for he was very cheerful. Putting his head forth from the window for a puff at a sand-hill, which was his prime luxury in a morning, he said to Wassamo:

"Son-in-law, you have been very patient with our long absence from your company, and you shall be rewarded. In a few days you may start with your wife to visit your relations. You can be absent one year, but at the end of that time, you must return. When you get to your home village, you must first go in alone. Leave your wife at a short distance from the lodge, and when you are welcome, then send for her. When there, do not be surprised that she disappears whenever you hear it thunder." He added, with a sly look, "That old Island Spirit has a brother down in that part of the country. You will prosper in all things, for my daughter is very diligent. All the time that you pass in sleep, she will be at work. The distance is short to your village. A path leads directly to it, and when you get there, do not forget my wants as I stated to you before.''

Wassamo promised obedience to these directions, and at the appointed time set out in company with his wife. They traveled on a pleasant course, his wife leading the way, until they reached a rising ground.

At the highest point of this ground, she said, ''We shall soon get to your country.''

It suddenly became broad day, as they came upon a high bank. Then they passed, unwet, for a short distance under the lake and presently emerged from the water at the sand-banks, just off the shore where Wassamo had set his nets on the night when he had been borne away by the two strange females.

Wassamo now left his wife sheltered in a neighboring wood, while he advanced toward the village alone. When he turned the first point of land by the lake he beheld his cousin as he walked the shore, musing sadly, and from time to time breaking forth in mournful cries.

With the speed of lightning the cousin rushed forward. ''Wassamo! Wassamo!'' he cried, ''is it indeed you? Whence have you come, oh, my cousin?''

They fell upon each other's necks and wept aloud. And then, without further delay or question, the cousin ran off with breathless despatch to the village. He seemed like a shadow upon the open ground, he sped so fast.

He entered the lodge where sat the mother of Wassamo in mourning for her son. ''Hear me,'' said the cousin. "I have seen him whom you accuse me of having killed. He will be here even while we speak."

He had scarcely uttered these words when the whole village was astir in an instant. All ran out and strained their eyes to catch the first view of him whom they had thought dead. And when Wassamo came forward, they at first fell from him as though he had been in truth one returned from the Spiritland. He entered the lodge of his parents. They saw that it was Wassamo, living, breathing and as they had ever known him. And joy lit up the lodge-circle as though a new fire had been kindled in the eyes of his friends and kinsfolk.

He related all that had happened to him from the moment of his leaving the temporary night-lodge with the flame on his head. He told them of the strange land in which he had sojourned during his absence. He added to his mother, apart from the company, that he was married, and that he had left his wife at a short distance from the village.

She went out immediately in search of her; they soon found her in the wood, and all the women in the village conducted her in honor to the lodge of her new relations. The Indian people were astonished at her beauty, at the whiteness of her skin, and still more, that she was able to talk with them in their own language.

The village was happy, and the feast went on as long as the supply held out. All were delighted to make the acquaintance of the old Sand-Spirit's daughter; and as they had heard that he was a magician and guardian of great power, the tobacco which he had sent for by his son-in-law came in great abundance with every visitor.

The summer and fall which Wassamo thus passed with his parents and the people of his tribe were prosperous with all the country.

The cousin of Wassamo recovered heart and sang once more his sad or mirthful chants, just as the humor was upon him; but he kept close by Wassamo and watched him in all his movements. He made it a point to ask many questions of the country he came from; some of which his cousin replied to, but others he left entirely unanswered.

At every thunderstorm, as the old Sand-Spirit had foreboded, the wife of Wassamo disappeared, much to the astonishment of her Indian company. And to their greater wonder she was never idle, night or day.

When the winter came on, Wassamo prepared for her a comfortable lodge to which she withdrew for her long sleep; and he gave notice to his friends that they must not disturb her, as she would not be with them again until the spring returned.

Before lying down, she said to her husband, "No one but yourself must pass on this side of the lodge."

The winter passed away with snows outside, and sports and stories in the lodge; and when the sap of the maple began to flow, the wife of Wassamo wakened and immediately set about work as before. She helped at the maple-trees with the others; and as if luck were in her presence, the sugar-harvest was greater than had been ever known in all that region.

The gifts of tobacco after this came in even more freely than they had at first; and as each giver brought his bundle to the lodge of Wassamo, he asked for the usual length of life, for success as a hunter, and for a plentiful supply of food. They particularly desired that the sand-hills might be kept quiet, so that their lands might be moist and their eyes clear of dust to sight the game.

Wassamo replied that he would mention each of their requests to his father-in-law.

The tobacco was stored in sacks, and on the outside of the skins, that there might be no mistake as to their wants, each one who had given tobacco had painted and marked in distinct characters the totem or family emblem of his family and tribe. These the old Sand-Spirit could read at his leisure and do what he thought best for each of his various petitioners.

When the time for his return arrived, Wassamo warned his people that they should not follow him or attempt to take note how he disappeared. He then took the moose-skin sacks filled with tobacco and bade farewell to all but Netawis. The latter insisted on the privilege of attending Wassamo and his wife for a distance, and when they reached the sand-banks he expressed the strongest wish to proceed with them on their journey. Wassamo told him that it could not be; that only spirits could exert the necessary power, and that there were no such spirits at hand.

They then took an affectionate leave of each other, Wassamo enjoining upon his cousin, at risk of his life, not to look back when he had once started to return.

The cousin, sore at heart but constrained to obey, parted from them; and as he walked sadly away, he heard a gliding noise as of the sound of waters that were cleaved.

He returned home and told his friends that Wassamo and his wife had disappeared, but that he knew not how. No one doubted his word in anything now.

Wassamo with his wife soon reached their home at the hills. The old Sand-Spirit was in excellent health and delighted to see them. He hailed their return with open arms; and he opened his arms so very wide, that when he closed them he not only embraced Wassamo and his wife, but all of the tobacco-sacks which they had brought with them.

The requests of the Indian people were made known to him; he replied that he would attend to all, but that he must first invite his friends to smoke with him. Accordingly he at once despatched his pipe-bearer and confidential aid to summon various Spirits of his acquaintance, and set the time for them to come.

Meanwhile he had a word of advice for his son-in-law, Wassamo. "My son," said he, "some of these

Manitos that I have asked to come here are of a very wicked temper, and I warn you especially of that Island Spirit who wished to marry my daughter. He is a very bad-hearted Monedo, and would like to do you harm. Some of the company, however, you will find to be very friendly. A caution for you. When they come in, do you sit close by your wife; if you do not, you will be lost. She only can save you; for those who are expected to come are so powerful that they will otherwise draw you from your seat and toss you out of the lodge as though you were a feather. You have only to observe my words and all will be well.''

Wassamo took heed to what the Old Spirit said and answered that he would obey.

About midday the company began to assemble; and such a company Wassamo had never looked on before. There were Spirits from all parts of the country; such strange-looking persons, and in dresses so wild and outlandish! One entered who smiled on him. This, Wassamo was informed, was a Spirit who had charge of the affairs of a tribe in the North, and he was as pleasant and cheery a Spirit as one would wish to see. Soon after, Wassamo heard a great rumbling and roaring, as of waters tumbling over rocks; and presently, with a vast bluster, and fairly shaking the lodge with his deep-throated hail of welcome to the old Sand-Spirit, in rolled another, who was the Guardian Spirit and special director of a great cataract or water-fall not far off.

Then came with crashing steps the owner of several whirlwinds, which were in the habit of raging about in the neighboring country. And following this one glided in a sweet-spoken, gentle-faced little Spirit, who was understood to represent a summer gale that was accustomed to blow in at the lodge-doors, toward evening, and to be particularly well disposed toward young lovers.

The last to appear was a great rocky-headed fellow; and he was twice as stony in his manners. He swaggered and strided in, and raised such a commotion with his great green blanket when he shook it, that Wassamo was nearly taken off his feet; and it was only by main force that he was able to cling by his wife. This, which was the last to enter, was that wicked Island Spirit, who looked grimly enough at Wassamo's wife as he passed in.

Soon after, the old Sand-Spirit, who was a great speech-maker, arose and addressed the assembly.

"Brothers," he said, "I have invited you to partake with me of the offerings made by the mortals on earth, which have been brought by our relation," pointing to Wassamo. "Brothers, you see their wishes and desires plainly set forth here," laying his hand upon the figured moose-skins. "The offering is worthy of our consideration. Brothers, I see noth-

ing on my part to hinder our granting their requests;
they do not appear to be unreasonable. Brothers,
the offer is gratifying. It is tobacco—an article which
we have lacked until we scarcely knew how to use our
pipes. Shall we grant their requests? One thing
more I would say. Brothers, it is this: There is my
son-in-law; he is mortal. I wish to detain him with
me, and it is with us jointly to make him one of us."

"Hoke! hoke!" ran though the whole company of
Spirits, and "Hoke! hoke!" they cried again. And
it was understood that the petitioners were to have all
they asked, and that Wassamo was thenceforward
fairly accepted as a member of the great family of
Spirits.

As a wedding-gift the Old Spirit promised his son-
in-law one request, which should be promptly granted.

"Let there be no sand-squalls among my father's
people for three months to come," said Wassamo.

"So shall it be," answered the old Sand-Spirit.

The tobacco was now divided in equal shares among
the company. They filled their pipes—and huge pipes
they were! And such clouds they blew, that they
rushed forth out of the lodge and brought on night
in all the country round about, several hours before
its time.

After a time passed in silence, the Spirits rose up,
and bearing off their tobacco-sacks, went smoking
through the country, losing themselves in their own
fog, till a late hour in the morning, when all of their

pipes being burned out, each departed on his own business.

The very next day the old Sand-Spirit, who was very much pleased with the turn affairs had taken at his entertainment, addressed Wassamo:

"Son-in-law, I have made up my mind to allow you another holiday as an acknowledgment of the handsome manner in which you acquitted yourself of your embassy. You may visit your parents and relatives once more, to tell them that their wishes are granted and to take your leave of them forever. You can never, after, visit them again."

Wassamo at once set out, reached his people, and was heartily welcomed.

They asked for his wife, and Wassamo informed them that she had tarried at home to look after a son, a fine little Sand-Spirit, who had been born to them since his return.

Having delivered all of his messages and passed a happy time, Wassamo said, "I must now bid you all farewell forever."

His parents and friends raised their voices in loud lamentation; they clung to him, and as a special favor, which he could now grant, being himself a spirit, he allowed them to accompany him to the sand-banks.

They all seated themselves to watch his last farewell. The day was mild, the sky clear, not a cloud appearing to dim the heavens, or a breath of wind to ruffle the tranquil waters. A perfect silence fell upon the company. They gazed with eager eyes fastened on Wassamo, as he waded out into the water, waving his hands. They saw him descend, more and more, into the depths. They beheld the waves close over his head, and a loud and piercing wail went up which rent the sky.

They looked again; a red flame, as if the sun had glanced on a billow, lighted the spot for an instant; but the Feather of Flames, Wassamo of the Fire-Plume, had disappeared from home and kindred and the familiar paths of his youth, forever.

XVIII

THE LITTLE BOY-MAN

A BOY remarkable for the smallness of his stature lived alone with his sister in a little lodge on a lake shore. Around their habitation were scattered many large rocks, and it had a very wild and out-of-the-way look.

The boy grew no larger as he advanced in years, and yet, small as he was, he had a big spirit of his own and loved dearly to play the master in the lodge. One day in winter he told his sister to make him a ball to play with, as he meant to have some sport along the shore on the clear ice. When she handed him the ball, his sister cautioned him not to go too far.

He laughed at her and posted off in high glee, throwing his ball before him and running after it at full speed; and he went as fast as his ball. At last the ball flew to a great distance, and he after it. When he had run forward for some time, he saw what seemed four dark spots upon the ice straight before him.

When he came up to the shore he was surprised to see four large, tall men lying on the ice, spearing fish. They were four brothers, who looked exactly alike.

As the little boy-man approached them, the nearest looked up, and in his turn was surprised to see such a tiny being. Turning to his brothers, he said:

"Tia! look! see what a little fellow is here."

The three others thereupon looked up, too, and seeing these four faces, as alike as if they had been one, the little spirit or boy-man said to himself:

"Four in one! What a time they must have in choosing their hunting-shirts!"

After they had all stared for a moment at the boy, they covered their heads, intent in searching for fish. The boy thought to himself:

"These four-faces fancy that I am to be put off without notice because I am so little and they are so broad and long. They shall find out. I may find a way to teach them that I am not to be treated so lightly."

After the men were covered up, the boy-man, looking sharply about, saw that among them they had caught one large trout, which was lying just by their side. Stealing along, he slyly seized it, and placing his fingers in the gills and tossing his ball before him, he ran off at full speed.

They heard the pattering of his little steps upon the ice, and when the four looked up all together, they saw their fine trout sliding away at a great rate, as if of itself, the boy being so small that he could not be distinguished from the fish.

"See!" they cried out, "our fish is running away on the dry land!"

When they stood up they could just see, over the fish's head, that it was the boy-man who was carrying it off.

The little spirit reached the lodge, and having left the trout at the door, he told his sister to go out and bring in the fish he had brought home.

She exclaimed, "Where could you have got it? I hope you have not stolen it."

"Oh," he replied, "I found it on the ice. It was caught in our lake. Have we no right to a little lake of our own? I shall claim all the fish that come out of its waters."

"How," the sister asked again, "could you have got it there?"

"No matter," said the boy; "go and cook it."

It was as much as the girl could do to drag the great trout within doors. Then she cooked it, and its flavor was so delicious that she asked no more questions as to how he had come by it.

The next morning the little spirit or boy-man set off as he had the day before.

He made all sorts of sport with his ball as he frolicked along—high over his head he would toss it; straight up into the air; then far before him; and again, in mere merriment of spirit, he would send it bounding back, as if he had plenty of speed and enough to spare in running back after it. And the ball leaped and bounced about and glided through the air as if it were a live thing, enjoying the sport as much as the boy-man himself.

When he came within hail of the four large men, who were fishing there every day, he cast his ball with such force that it rolled into the ice-hole about which they were busy. The boy, standing on the shore of the lake, called out:

"Four-in-one, pray hand me my ball."

"No, indeed," they answered, setting up a grim laugh which curdled their four dark faces all at once, "we will not"; and with their fishing-spears they thrust the ball under the ice.

"Good!" said the boy-man, "we shall see."

Saying which he rushed upon the four brothers and thrust them at one push into the water. His ball bounded back to the surface, and, picking it up, he ran off, tossing it before him in his own sportive way. Outstripping it in speed, he soon reached home and remained within till the next morning.

The four brothers, rising up from the water at the same time, dripping and wroth, roared out in one voice a terrible threat of vengeance, which they promised to execute the next day. They knew the boy's speed, and that they could by no means overtake him.

Betimes in the morning, the four brothers were stirring in their lodge and getting ready to look after their revenge.

Their old mother, who lived with them, begged them not to go.

"Better," said she, "now that your clothes are dry, to think no more of the ducking, than to go and all four of you get your heads broken, as you surely will; for that boy is a monedo or he could not perform such feats as he does."

Her sons, however, paid no heed to this wise advice. Raising a great war-cry, which frightened the birds overhead nearly out of their feathers, they started for the boy's lodge among the rocks.

The little spirit or boy-man heard them roaring forth their threats as they approached, but he did not appear to be disquieted in the least. His sister as yet had heard nothing; after a while she thought she could distinguish the noise of snowshoes on the snow, at a distance, but rapidly advancing. She looked out, and seeing the four large men coming straight to their lodge she was in great fear. Running in, she exclaimed:

"He is coming, four times as strong as ever!" for she supposed that the one man whom her brother had offended had become so angry as to make four of himself in order to wreak his vengeance.

The boy-man said, "Why do you mind them? Give me something to eat."

"How can you think of eating at such a time?" she replied.

"Do as I request you, and be quick."

She then gave the little spirit his dish, and he commenced eating.

Just then the brothers came to the door.

"See!" cried the sister, "the man with four heads!"

The brothers were about to lift the curtain at the door, when the boy-man turned his dish upside down, and immediately the door was closed with a stone. The four brothers set to work upon this and hammered with their clubs with great fury, until at length they succeeded in making a slight opening. One of the brothers presented his face at this little window and rolled his eye about at the boy-man in a very threatening way.

The little spirit, who, when he had closed the door, had returned to his meal and gone on quietly eating, took up his bow and arrow which lay by his side, and let fly the shaft. It struck the man in the head, and he fell back. The boy-man merely called out, "Number one," as he fell, and went on with his meal.

In a moment a second face, just like the first, presented itself; and as he raised his bow, his sister said to him:

"What is the use? You have killed that man already."

Little spirit fired his arrow—the man fell—he called out, "Number two," and continued his meal.

The two others of the four brothers were despatched in the same quiet way and counted off as "Number three" and "Number four."

After they were all well disposed of in this way, the boy-man directed his sister to go out and see them. She presently ran back, saying:

"There are four of them."

"Of course," the boy-man answered, "and there always shall be four of them."

Going out himself, the boy-man raised the brothers to their feet, and giving each a push, one with his face to the East, another to the West, a third to the South, and the last to the North, he sent them off to wander about the earth; and whenever you see four men just alike, they are the four brothers whom the little spirit or boy-man despatched upon their travels.

But this was not the last display of the boy-man's power.

When spring came on, and the lake began to sparkle in the morning sun, the boy-man said to his sister:

"Make me a new set of arrows and a bow."

Although he provided for their support, the little spirit never performed household or hard work of any kind, and his sister obeyed.

When she had made the weapons, which, though they were very small, were beautifully wrought and of the best stuff the field and wood could furnish, she again cautioned him not to shoot into the lake.

"She thinks," said the boy-man to himself, "I can see no farther into the water than she. My sister shall learn better."

Regardless of her warnings, he on purpose discharged a shaft into the lake and waded out into the water till he got to its depth. Then he paddled about for his arrow, so as to call the attention of his sister, as if to show that he hardily braved her advice.

She hurried to the shore, calling on him to return; but instead of heeding her, he cried out:

"You of the red fins, come and swallow me!"

Although his sister did not clearly understand whom her brother was addressing, she too called out:

"Don't mind the foolish boy!"

The boy-man's order seemed to be best attended to, for immediately a monstrous fish came and swallowed him. Before disappearing entirely, catching a glimpse of his sister standing in despair upon the shore, the boy-man hallooed out to her:

"Me-zush-ke-zin-ance!"

She wondered what he meant. At last it occurred to her that it must be an old moccasin. She accordingly ran to the lodge, brought a moccasin, tied it to a string attached to a tree, and quickly cast it into the water.

The great fish said to the boy-man under water:

"What is that floating?"

To which the boy-man replied:

"Go, take hold of it, swallow it as fast as you can; it is a great delicacy."

The fish darted toward the old shoe and swallowed it, making of it a mere mouthful.

The boy-man laughed to himself but said nothing,

till the fish was fairly caught; when he took hold of the line and began to pull himself ashore in his fish-carriage.

The sister, who was watching all this time, opened wide her eyes as the huge fish came up and up upon the shore; and she opened them still more when the fish seemed to speak, and she heard from within a voice, saying, "Make haste and release me from this nasty place."

It was her brother's voice, which she was accustomed to obey; and she made haste with her knife to open a door in the side of the fish, from which the boy-man presently leaped forth. He lost no time in ordering her to cut up the fish and dry it; telling her that their spring supply of meat was now provided.

The sister now began to believe that her brother was an extraordinary boy; yet she was not altogether satisfied in her mind that he was greater than the rest of the world.

They sat one evening in the lodge, musing with each other in the dark, by the light of each other's eyes, when the sister said:

"My brother, it is strange that you, who can do so much, are no wiser than the Ko-ko, who gets all his light from the moon; which shines or not, as it pleases."

"And is not that light enough?" asked the little spirit.

"Quite enough," the sister replied. "If it would

but come within the lodge and not sojourn out in the tree-tops and among the clouds.''

"We will have a light of our own, sister," said the boy-man; and, casting himself upon a mat by the door, he commenced singing:

> Fire-fly, fire-fly, bright little thing,
> Light me to bed and my song I will sing;
> Give me your light, as you fly o'er my head,
> That I may merrily go to my bed.
>
> Give me your light o'er the grass as you creep,
> That I may joyfully go to my sleep;
> Come, little fire-fly, come little beast,
> Come! and I'll make you to-morrow a feast.
>
> Come, little candle, that flies as I sing,
> Bright little fairy-bug, night's little king;
> Come and I'll dream, as you guide me along;
> Come and I'll pay you, my bug, with a song.

As the boy-man chanted this call, the fire-flies came into the lodge, first one by one, then in couples, till at last, swarming in little armies, they lighted the lodge with a thousand sparkling lamps, just as the stars were lighting the mighty hollow of the sky without.

The faces of the sister and brother shone upon each other from their opposite sides of the lodge with a kindly gleam of mutual trustfulness; and never more from that hour did a doubt of each other darken their little household.

XIX

WUNZH, THE FATHER OF INDIAN CORN

IN time past—we cannot tell exactly how many, many years ago—a poor Indian was living with his wife and children in a beautiful part of the country. He was not only poor, but he had the misfortune to be inexpert in procuring food for his family, and his children were all too young to give him any assistance.

Although of a lowly condition and straitened in his circumstances, he was a man of kind and contented disposition. He was always thankful to the Great Spirit for everything he received. He even stood in the door of his lodge to bless the birds that flew past in the summer evenings; although, if he had been of a complaining temper, he might have repined that they were not rather spread upon the table for his evening meal.

The same gracious and sweet disposition was inherited by his eldest son, who had now arrived at the proper age to undertake the ceremony of the fast to learn what kind of a spirit would be his guide and guardian through life.

Wunzh, for this was his name, had been an obedient boy from his infancy—pensive, thoughtful, and gentle —so that he was beloved by the whole family.

As soon as the first buds of spring appeared and the

delicious fragrance of the young year began to sweeten the air, his father, with the help of his younger brothers, built for Wunzh the customary little lodge at a retired spot some distance from their own, where he would not be disturbed during the solemn rite.

To prepare himself, Wunzh sought to clear his heart of every evil thought and to think of nothing that was not good, and beautiful, and kindly.

That he might store his mind with pleasant ideas for his dreams, for the first few days he amused himself by walking in the woods and over the mountains, examining the early plants and flowers.

As he rambled far and wide through the wild country, he felt a strong desire to know how the plants and herbs and berries grew, without any aid from man, and why it was that some kinds were good to eat, and that others were possessed of medicinal or poisonous power.

After he had become too languid from fasting to walk about, and confined himself strictly to the lodge, he recalled these thoughts. Turning them in his mind, he wished he could dream of something that would prove a benefit to his father and family, and to all others of his fellow-creatures.

"True," thought Wunzh, "the Great Spirit made all things, and it is to him that we owe our lives. Could he not make it easier for us to get our food than by hunting animals and taking fish? I must try to find this out in my visions."

On the third day Wunzh became weak and faint, and lay flat in a kind of stupor. Suddenly he fancied that a bright light came in at the lodge door, and ere he was aware, he saw a handsome young man, with a complexion of the softest and purest white, coming down from the sky and advancing toward him.

The beautiful stranger was richly and gaily dressed, having on a great many garments of green and yellow colors, but differing in their deeper or lighter shades. He had a plume of waving feathers on his head, and all his motions were graceful, reminding Wunzh of the deep green of the summer grass, the clear amber of the summer sky, and the gentle blowing of the summer wind. As Wunzh gazed at his visitor, he paused on a little mound of earth just before the door of the lodge.

"I am sent to you, my friend," said this celestial visitor, in a voice most soft and musical to listen to, "I am sent to you by that Great Spirit who made all things in the sky and on the earth. He has seen and knows your motives in fasting. He sees that it is from a kind and benevolent wish to do good to your people and to procure a benefit for them; and that you do not seek for strength in war, or the praise of the men of the bloody hand. So I am sent to instruct you and to show you how you can do your kindred good."

He then told Wunzh to arise and to prepare to wrestle with him, as it was only by this means that he could hope to succeed in his desires.

Wunzh knew how weak he was from fasting, but the voice of the stranger was cheery and put such a courage in his heart, that he promptly sprang up, determined to die rather than fail.

He began the trial, and after a long-sustained struggle, was almost overpowered, when the beautiful stranger said:

"My friend, it is enough for once; I will come again to try you," and smiling on him, he returned through the air in the same direction in which he had come.

The next day, although Wunzh saw how sweetly the wild-flowers bloomed upon the slopes and the birds warbled from the woodland, he longed to see the celestial visitor and to hear his voice.

To his great joy he reappeared at the same hour, toward the going down of the sun, and re-challenged Wunzh to a trial of strength.

The brave Wunzh felt that his strength of body was even less than on the day before, but the courage of his mind seemed to grow. Observing this, and how Wunzh put his whole heart into the struggle, the stranger again spoke to him in the words he used before, adding:

"To-morrow will be your last trial. Be strong, my friend, for this is the only way in which you can overcome me and obtain the boon you seek."

The light which shone after him as he left Wunzh was brighter than before.

On the third day he came again and renewed the

struggle. Very faint in body was poor Wunzh, but he was stronger at heart than ever, and determined to prevail now or perish. He put forth his utmost powers, and after a contest more severe than either of the others, the stranger ceased his efforts and declared himself conquered.

For the first time he entered Wunzh's little fasting-lodge, and sitting down beside the youth, he began to deliver his instructions to him and to inform him in what manner he should proceed to take advantage of his victory.

"You have won your desire of the Great Spirit," said the beautiful stranger. "You have wrestled manfully. To-morrow will be the seventh day of your fasting. Your father will give you food to strengthen you, and as it is the last day of trial you will prevail. I know this, and now tell you what you must do to benefit your family and your people. To-morrow," he repeated, "I shall meet you and wrestle with you for the last time. As soon as you have prevailed against me, you will strip off my garments and throw me down, clean the earth of roots and weeds, make it soft, and bury me in the spot. When you have done this, leave my body in the earth and do not disturb it, but come at times to visit the place, to see whether I have come to life, and above all be careful never to let the grass or weeds grow upon my grave. Once a month cover me with fresh earth. If you follow these my instructions you will accomplish your object of

doing good to your fellow-creatures by teaching them
the knowledge I now teach you.''

He then shook Wunzh by the hand and disappeared,
but he was gone so soon that Wunzh could not tell
what direction he took.

In the morning, Wunzh's father came to his lodge
with some slight refreshments, saying:

"My son, you have fasted long enough. If the
Great Spirit will favor you, he will do it now. It is
seven days since you have tasted food, and you must
not sacrifice your life. The Master of Life does not
require that.''

"My father,'' replied Wunzh, "wait till the sun goes
down. I have a particular reason for extending my
fast to that hour.''

"Very well,'' said the old man, "I shall wait till
the hour arrives, and you shall be inclined to eat.''

At his usual hour of appearing, the beautiful sky-
visitor returned, and the trial of strength was renewed.
Although he had not availed himself of his father's
offer of food, Wunzh felt that new strength had been
given him. His heart was mighty within him to
achieve some great purpose. Within the bosom of the
brave Wunzh courage was like the eagle that spreads
his wings within the tree-top for a great flight.

He grasped his challenger with supernatural
strength, threw him down, and, mindful of his instructions, tore away his beautiful garments and plume.
Finding him dead, he immediately buried him on the

spot, using all the precautions he had been told of, and very confident was Wunzh, all the time, that his friend would again come to life.

Wunzh now returned to his father's lodge, where he was warmly welcomed. For as it had been appointed to him during the days of his fasting to walk apart, he had not been permitted to see any human face save that of his father, the representative to the little household upon earth of the great Father of all people.

Wunzh partook sparingly of the meal that had been prepared for him, and once more mingled in the cares and sports of the family. But he never for a moment forgot the grave of his friend. He carefully visited it throughout the spring, weeded out the grass, and kept the ground in a soft and pliant state; and sometimes, when the brave Wunzh thought of his friend that was gone from his sight, he dropped a tear upon the earth where he lay.

Watching and tending and moistening the earth with his tears, it was not long before Wunzh saw the tops of green plumes coming through the ground; and the more faithful he was in obeying his instructions in keeping the ground in order and in cherishing the memory of his friend, the faster they grew. He was, however, careful to conceal all these things from his father.

Days and weeks had passed in this way; the summer was drawing toward a close, when one day Wunzh invited his father to follow him to the quiet and lonesome spot of his former fast.

The little fasting-lodge had been removed and the weeds kept from growing on the circle where it had stood; but in its place rose a tall and graceful plant, surmounted with nodding plumes, stately leaves, and golden clusters. There was in its aspect and bearing the deep green of the summer grass, the clear amber of the summer sky, and the gentle blowing of the summer wind.

"It is my friend!" shouted Wunzh, "it is the friend of all mankind. It is Mondawmin: it is our Indian Corn! We need no longer rely on hunting alone, for as long as this gift is cherished and taken care of, the ground itself will give us a living."

He then pulled an ear.

"See, my father," said he, "this is what I fasted for. The Great Spirit has listened to my voice and sent us something new. Henceforth our people will not alone depend upon the chase or upon the waters."

Wunzh then communicated to his father the instructions given to him by the stranger. He told him that the broad husks must be torn away, as he had pulled off the stranger's garments in his wrestling. Then he showed him how the ear must be held before the fire till the outer skin becomes brown, while all the milk is retained in the grain.

The whole family, in high spirits and deeply grateful, assisted in a feast on the newly grown ears of corn.

So came that mighty blessing into the world, and we owe all of those beautiful fields of healthful grain to the dream of the brave boy Wunzh.

THE END